A SECRET IN THE BAY

CHASING TIDES BOOK TWO

FIONA BAKER

JOIN MY NEWSLETTER

If you love beachy, feel-good women's fiction, sign up to receive my newsletter, where you'll get free books, exclusive bonus content, and info on my new releases and sales!

CHAPTER ONE

Luke Ward breathed a sigh of relief as he tucked his laptop into his backpack and toed into his sneakers. The TSA line at the airport hadn't been as long as he'd seen it before, but traveling with all of his gadgets made getting through security a bit of a hassle. He had to take everything out and sort it into baskets. And inevitably, he'd forget to take something out and his bag had to be searched, just as it had been today.

He expected it, though, and didn't mind at the end of the day. He would have felt naked without all of his gear. His hands always itched to work with something, to take things apart and put them back together once he figured out how they worked.

He fully intended to soak in the beauty of

Blueberry Bay that summer, but keeping up with his repair skills in his down time away from his aunt Sandy and uncle Daniel's grocery store wasn't going to hurt. The process that was so frustrating to most people was relaxing to him, and always had been. It had driven his parents crazy when he was a kid. He'd take apart anything he could get his hands on, just to see how it worked.

Eventually they started to swing by second-hand shops just to get him something that he could fix without costing them hundreds of dollars. Soon he learned he had a knack for fixing things that people thought were broken for good. Selling refurbished electronics he'd picked up from various stores gave him a steady income of spending money in high school and college. He saved half of it for his eventual business and used the other half as spending money.

The thought of running his own business gave him a small rush every time. He didn't mind working for others, but the idea of building something himself, something he could call his own, was incredibly appealing and had been since he was young. Sandy had inspired him—she had built up her store alongside her husband and now it was the go-to place for groceries or anything else someone might need in Blueberry Bay. It was hard work getting there, but it was satisfying.

He glanced up at the signs for the various gates and found the one he was looking for: a flight from Indianapolis to Boston. It was at the far end of the terminal and he had plenty of time before boarding, so he took his time. He wove through the crowds of people, stepping into a gift shop and balking at the price of a bottle of water. It wasn't even sparkling water, just plain old water.

He decided against buying any water, but he was a graduate student and coffee got him through the hardest days. He'd gotten up early to finish packing and make the hour long drive from Bloomington to the Indianapolis airport, so he desperately needed a cup. The line to the coffee shop was easy to spot. It wound around the food court, so he stood at the end. It went by faster than he anticipated. Forking over six dollars for a large coffee with cream and sugar hurt, but he forgot all about the blow to his graduate student budget once he took his first sip.

Eventually he got to his gate and sat down, excitement buzzing through his veins as planes pulled up and away from the various gates. Finishing all of is final projects lifted a huge weight off of his shoulders and he was glad to get a chance to unwind.

He pulled out his worn paperback and thumbed through it. How long had it been since he read for pleasure? Way too long. The flight from Indianapolis to Boston was a little over two hours, then he had to take a ferry to get to Blueberry Bay. He had more time than he'd had in ages, so he opened the book and started reading. Before he knew it, it was time to board.

He polished off his coffee and tossed the cup away before he boarded. The airplane was big, not that that meant a lot. His long legs didn't have enough room to fit comfortably, but he'd gotten a window seat. The view as the plane took off almost made up for the lack of leg space. The world got smaller and smaller until everything was made up of green dots and empty fields.

He smiled to himself. Summers in Blueberry Bay were always filled with the unexpected, and he was excited to see what this year would bring.

* * *

"Two BLTs, one without the T," Hannah Jenkins called back to her father, Willis, who was hard at work on the lunch rush at their restaurant, The Crab.

Willis peeked through the service window, raising an eyebrow at the order as if to ask, *what's the point of a BLT without one of the primary ingredients?*

Hannah bit the inside of her cheek to hide her smile. There was always one customer who had an order like that. She had been working at The Crab with her dad since she was a teenager, so she had seen it all. Today wasn't an unusual Tuesday by any means.

She went back to the register with a smile, steadily taking the lunch rush orders. The Crab specialized in sandwiches, so it was the go-to spot for most of Blueberry Bay's lunch hour. She'd been working there for so long that she hardly blinked as she went between the register, answering questions about the menu, and cleaning up tables in between customers. Eventually it slowed down enough for her to take a breath and tidy up behind the counter.

"Hi, welcome to The Crab!" Hannah said to a couple who had just walked in. She could clearly tell they were tourists. She knew most of the people who came regularly, and she didn't recognize these people. They were in their early twenties, just like Hannah, and were dressed up more than the locals too. If she had to guess, they were from Boston or

New York City, where the vast majority of tourists to their town came from. "What can I get for you guys?"

"What's good? We've never been here before," the woman said, absently playing with the row of earrings lining her ear.

"Depends on what you're looking for. Do you want something light, or something a little heavier?" Hannah looked up at the menu board even though she knew everything on the menu plus the specials by heart. "Our crab roll is one of our customer favorites, just light enough but not so light that you don't feel like you've eaten. The crab is super fresh, just arrived this morning. But if you want something that'll stick to your ribs more, our chicken cutlet sandwich and fries will keep you full for a while. It's not greasy at all, but it's enormous. Definitely for a big appetite or if you want to split something."

The man in the couple laughed. He also had a few earrings, plus a septum piercing under his nose.

"I feel like having a big sandwich and passing out on the beach is exactly what I'm after," he said. "I'll try the chicken sandwich and fries."

"And I'll have the crab roll since I want to read instead of falling into a food coma," the woman said. "With the homemade chips on the side."

"Gotcha." Hannah plugged in their orders. "Anything to drink? We have some local beers and ciders right now. We serve harder drinks in the evening. And we have iced tea, water, sodas..."

"Iced tea sounds nice," the woman said.

Hannah nodded and plugged in their orders before calling them back to Willis, more out of habit than anything. She'd upgraded their system so it printed out a ticket in the kitchen a few years back.

"This place is so cute," the woman said, wandering along the shop. "Even cuter than the reviews said. How long have you been working here?"

"Since I was a teenager. My dad—he's back there —owns the place." Hannah stacked some napkins and put them on the utensils stand. "Are you guys visiting from out of town?"

"Yep! From Boston," the man said, following the woman. "We needed an escape from the city. It looks like we're not alone."

"Definitely not," Hannah said. July was always packed with tourists. "We love for people to visit."

"People are so friendly here." The woman smiled and ran her fingers along copies of the local newspaper, *The Outlet*. After glancing at the headline, she picked up a copy.

"*The Outlet* is great," Hannah said. "If you ever need to find out anything that's going on, it'll have it."

"Cool." The woman thumbed through it and looked up at her companion. "Maybe we can look through here to find things to do."

They fell into their own conversation, talking about finding time to rest and recharge their creative spirits while they were away. Hannah was curious, but she didn't want to pry. Based on the context, they were musicians.

Hannah poured the couple's drinks, burning with curiosity. She had taught herself piano and loved to play. What was life like as a full-time musician? She imagined something glamorous, or at least glamorous in comparison to where she was today: meeting people from all over, traveling, performing for huge audiences. The tourists had an air of sophistication that suggested they'd be right at home doing all of that.

The couple's food came up and they went outside, leaving Hannah with a loose knot in her stomach for reasons she couldn't pinpoint.

The Crab was a second home to her and had been for years. It had been just her and her dad since her mother left when she was young, so she felt tied to the place. In the past, she had found comfort in that. She always had a place to go, a place that felt like home. But now it was starting to itch, just a little bit. Was there anything for her outside of Blueberry Bay? Maybe something with music?

She brushed those thoughts off, as she often did. She loved Blueberry Bay and always would, but she'd long accepted the fact that the things there and the people were just... ordinary. Sometimes a minor celebrity came through, but that was as exciting as it got. It was definitely not Boston or anything close to it.

Hannah finished tidying up, the end of the lunch crowd now settled with their food, and went to the back to help with prep for the dinner menu. They served similar dishes every single day, so she didn't have to think twice about what to do. She fell into the easy rhythm of chopping and checking ingredients until the bell above the door jingled.

"Be with you in a second!" Hannah called. She washed her hands and went out front, her heart flipping in her chest when she saw who had come in. "Oh, hi, Michael."

"Hi, Hannah."

Michael O'Neil looked like he had just come in off the waves. His dark hair was windswept off his handsome, tanned face. He was the one thing around Blueberry Bay that didn't feel ordinary to her. Something about the way he carried himself and talked to people made him feel like he had the answers without being arrogant. Like he'd seen enough of the world to know himself well and be secure in who he was.

He owned the most popular coffee shop in town, Tidal Wave Coffee. A lot of her friends from high school had worked there since he liked to employ local young people to give them a good first job for their resumes. On top of that, he was a pro surfer and was sponsored by major surf brands.

To Hannah, he was a movie star. Looks and all. Despite that, she wondered if he'd ever notice her. Sure, he was older than her, somewhere in his early thirties, but she always held onto a little hope. Couples had age differences all the time.

Then again, she was far from the only one in town with a little crush on him. Hannah was sure that some of the girls she knew who worked at Tidal Wave had gotten the job partially because Michael would be their boss. And wherever he went, eyes followed him.

"Um, what can I get you?" Hannah asked, stumbling over her words.

"I'll take a crab roll and chips. Plus an iced tea to go," Michael said.

"Gotcha." Her heart fluttered and she played with her necklace in the hopes that it would calm her down.

"Has it been busy today?" he asked as he paid.

"Yeah. I mean, sort of." Hannah felt her cheeks warm. Despite living in a seaside town, her skin was extremely fair, so every blush showed. "Just a regular Tuesday."

"Yeah. I swung by Tidal Wave and it was about the same. The waves were perfect, though."

"Yeah?" She had seen him surf before. He made it look so effortless. She knew how to surf and enjoyed it, but she wiped out a few times before managing to catch a wave. Luckily no one had recorded her flailing off her board and plunging into the water. She poured him some iced tea in a to-go cup.

"Yup. And the water is finally getting warmer." He smiled, making his already attractive face even more so. She loved the faint lines that appeared around his brown eyes.

"That's great." Any more eloquent replies escaped Hannah as their fingers brushed when she handed him his tea.

Her ability to think clearly didn't come back until Michael had his sandwich and was out the door. Hannah's heart finally slowed down and her shoulders sagged. Maybe next time she'd think of the right thing to say.

CHAPTER TWO

Alissa pushed her glasses up on her nose, then went right back to typing. Her latest article for *The Outlet*, the first of a few pieces on the upcoming Blueberry Bay Luau, was flowing out of her almost faster than she could type.

The event was over a month away, but she couldn't wait, even though she hadn't been before. People were going to come from out of town to enjoy the games, vendors, surfing, and of course, hula dancing. Blueberry Bay was a tight-knit community, so any event that brought everyone to the same place was bound to be fun.

She suppressed a smile, trying to imagine herself doing the hula. Even though she wasn't much of a dancer, she was more than willing to try it. These past few months had been a series of trying new things. If someone had told her that she would be living in a small town, working as the head reporter at a new and rapidly growing newspaper and magazine, she wouldn't have believed it.

But she was, and she was happier than she had been in a long time. Her happiness had come from one of the worst periods in her life. She'd gotten fired from what she'd thought was her dream job at *Epic News* and on a whim, she'd come to Blueberry Bay to figure out what she wanted to do next. Through a series of lucky happenstances, she'd found *The Outlet*, which was desperate for writers, and started working there. The beautiful Rhode Island scenery had inspired her to write again, a hobby long put aside because of the stresses of work, and now her debut novel was on shelves across the country.

She had taken to Blueberry Bay almost right away, finding joy in bonding with the locals, who embraced her. It was so different than being in Denver. It wasn't the biggest city by any means and the people were friendly, but there was an impermanence to it that she didn't find in Blueberry Bay. People didn't stop to linger in places or strike up conversations with people they saw regularly—two things Alissa had come to love about the town.

She bit her bottom lip, trying to think of the perfect way to end the article. After a few moments, it came to her, and she typed it out with flourish. The satisfaction of finishing an article was second to none.

"Hey." Her boss and boyfriend, Dane, appeared in the doorway and knocked on the frame.

Seeing him still made her heart flip-flop in her chest even though they had been together for a few months now. He was one of the most handsome men she'd ever seen, with thick auburn hair and fiercely intelligent green eyes. He had come from New York City and still dressed the part to some extent in his slacks and neatly tailored button-down shirt. But he had lost the tie and vest that he used to wear regularly. Alissa liked him either way.

Dane was one of the best things to happen to her since her move. He had been a crabby workaholic when they first met, barely able to crack a smile or see what Blueberry Bay had to offer. But now he had fallen in love with the town just as much as she had and had rediscovered why he loved writing too.

They had fun going out and exploring, but also just enjoying each other's company, curled up on the couch together with books. Sometimes getting him to relax took a little effort, but he was getting more and more willing to slow down the more she encouraged him.

"Hey! Perfect timing. I just finished my article on the luau." She tabbed over to her email and opened a new draft. "Let me send it to you."

"Nice work." He smiled. "Want to grab an early lunch with me to celebrate? I was thinking we could go to The Crab."

"That sounds perfect." Alissa attached the article to the email and sent it off to Dane. "I'm super hungry."

She gathered her purse and put it on her shoulder, leaving her office. Dane rested his hand on her back as they walked. Being with him felt so easy, but it was never boring. He kept her on her toes, but made her feel safe and secure at the same time.

"See you later, Josie," Dane said to his secretary, who was nibbling on a granola bar at her desk.

"Want us to bring you anything?" Alissa asked.

"No, I'm good! I just had The Crab last night. See you guys soon," Josie said.

Dane threaded his fingers in Alissa's and led her out the door and toward town.

The summer weather was just the kind that Alissa loved—hot, but not too humid. Sunny, but not so sunny that she felt like she was getting a sunburn if she was outside for more than two minutes. The air was crisp and clean in a different way than Denver's air was—the salt in the air, the presence of the ocean never far from any part of town.

She squeezed Dane's hand a little as they walked in comfortable silence. Just being next to Dane made her day a little brighter—the warmth of his hand, which never felt like too much, even on the warmest days, the familiar scent of his laundry soap and shampoo.

"Want to walk along the boardwalk since it's so nice?" Dane asked.

"Sure, I'd love to."

Dane steered them more to the right, where the boardwalk started. With the summer tourist season in full swing and school out, it was much busier than usual. Families wrangled their kids into swim shirts or lathered them in sunscreen as they refused to stay still, couples like them walked hand in hand, and the shops and restaurants along the boardwalk were busy with the lunch rush.

Alissa looked around, taking it all in. It wasn't nearly as busy as it could get on a Saturday afternoon, but it was still busy enough to make her feel excited.

"Oh, look at that!" Alissa said, gesturing out to

the edge of the beach. "A bunch of people are learning how to surf."

Dane stopped next to her and looked at the water too. An instructor was on his board on the sand, demonstrating how to hop up onto it. The students gave it a shot, struggling to do it even though the instructor had made it look easy.

"How cool!" Alissa looked to Dane. "I've always wondered what it would be like to surf. I can't imagine being that one with the ocean, you know?"

"It does sound difficult. The surfers in competition make it look so easy. But isn't it slippery? What if the wave isn't quite right?" Dane asked, wandering forward.

"Don't know. I'm guessing they teach you that." Alissa looked down the path and brightened. "Oh, look! They have surf lessons here. Wouldn't that be fun to try together?"

Dane let out a nervous laugh. "I would be more than willing to cheer you on from the beach, slathered in sunscreen and wearing a hat."

"Aw, come on. The wetsuits will keep you from burning." With his auburn hair and fair skin, he'd gotten a few rough sunburns despite all of the sunscreen he religiously applied when they were on the beach.

"True. But..." Dane shrugged. "Seriously, I would have a great time watching you learn."

Alissa's heart sank a tiny bit. Learning to surf did sound scary—even swimming out deeper into the water scared her if the water was rough—but it seemed like it could be exhilarating if she learned the basics. It was just the kind of activity that she wished Dane would try with her. Something new where things weren't tied into a neat bow.

But it wasn't that big of a deal. Even Alissa was slightly too intimidated to sign up for a lesson right then and there. So, she smiled and nudged him with her shoulder.

"Are you just saying that because it would be hilarious to watch me flop around like a seal in the water?" Alissa asked.

"Of course not." Dane laughed. "I just like to be near you when you're in your adventurous mode."

Alissa softened at that. Dane would always support her no matter what she did, but she wished he would dive in with her every once in a while. Maybe someday they could surf together.

* * *

Luke adjusted his backpack on his back as the ferry pulled into the port at Blueberry Bay. It was a perfect summer day, sunny with just a few clouds drifting across the sun to give them relief from the heat. The ocean was a rich, beautiful blue that made him want to dive right in, small islands breaking up the blue in the distance. He made his way toward the exit of the ferry, excitement building in his chest.

Blueberry Bay had the same small town charm that he remembered—everything seemed more intimate, like everyone, everywhere had each other's backs. The small tourists' station near the parking lot was overflowing with people, but he didn't need to go there today. He looked around the parking lot until he found his aunt Sandy Ryan and her husband, Daniel.

They were impossible to miss. Sandy was so petite that she barely reached her husband's shoulder, her blonde hair back in its usual braid. Daniel had his arm around her, his strong, broad frame a sharp contrast from his wife's. They both smiled when they spotted him.

"Hey!" Luke said when he got close enough.

"Hey!" Sandy pulled him into a hug. "Have you gotten taller since I saw you last?"

Luke snorted, then gave Daniel a hug. "No. I stopped growing a few years back, I think."

"I'm just shrinking then." Sandy sighed, a smile still on her face. It was an old running joke between them—Luke had been taller than Sandy since he was fourteen. "Ready to go?"

"Yeah. I'm wiped."

They walked to Daniel's SUV and piled inside, pulling off toward their home just outside of town. Luke rolled down the window a few inches to enjoy the salty ocean breeze on his face.

"Do you miss school yet?" Sandy asked, turning to look at him.

"Sort of." He had always loved school, which was why going to business school was a no brainer after he finished undergrad. "I miss learning and talking to my classmates. But I'm excited to finish my final year and finally have time to start my business."

His dream of starting his own electronics repair store had been nothing but a strong desire up until he was in undergrad, where it cemented in his brain as something he could actively start working toward. When people thought about technology, their minds instantly went to software and apps, but so many people gave up on fixing their gadgets, opting to buy new ones when theirs would be perfectly fine with a little tweaking.

His classes were the perfect opportunity to hone his skills. Every project was an opportunity to think of something he wanted his business to do, and his classmates were great sounding boards for his ideas. He couldn't wait for his final year so he could start the last stretch of his education and the beginning leg of building his business for real.

"Definitely. It takes a lot of time," Sandy said. "You're smart for not trying to do it all and burn yourself out in the process."

Luke nodded. He had watched Sandy build her store from the ground up over the years. Now it was so popular that they needed a lot more help than they had. That was where he came in.

"You should take a look at the laptop we use at the store," Daniel said, looking at his wife for a brief moment. "It's been glitchy. And yes, Sandy, it's my fault."

"I didn't say anything!" Sandy chuckled.

"What happened?" Luke asked.

"I bumped it with my hip and it fell. Luckily it only hit a rug and it worked just fine after that. But there's some software updates and whatnot that might be the culprit." Daniel shrugged his wide shoulders.

"Sure, I'd be happy to help," Luke said. Dropped laptops and other gadgets were pretty common fixes. And if it was a software issue, he could help them with that too—he'd learned a lot about it to keep himself well-rounded. "It's the least I can do since you guys are letting me stay with you this summer. I'm the one who owes you guys a favor."

* * *

"Look, Pearl," Caitlin said to her daughter, pulling her a bit closer. "The otters are holding hands!"

Pearl gasped in delight as she watched the otters floating across the pool on their backs in their enclosure. The otters were new to the Denver Aquarium, and were by far the most popular attraction of the day. Plus, it was a new addition. Visiting the aquarium was always one of Caitlin's favorite things to do with Pearl and her husband, James.

Except James wasn't there, at least not yet.

"So cute!" Pearl went on her tiptoes to see better. "Aren't they?"

Caitlin took Pearl's moment of distraction to look

down at her phone. Still no messages from James. The knot in Caitlin's stomach tightened more and she tried to take a deep breath to loosen it. It didn't work.

This morning Caitlin had asked him at least three times if he'd come to the aquarium with them, and each time he said yes in the hurried, vaguely passive way she'd become accustomed to by now.

He was supposed to have been there a half hour ago, and she hoped he was still on his way. The restaurant they owned and operated together was a good half hour from the aquarium and by then, she and Pearl would have been done with looking at everything.

He was still a loving father to Pearl—she never questioned that—but she just wished he was around more.

The restaurant took up so much of his time that Caitlin could hardly remember the last time they'd had an afternoon together as a family. When was it, before Thanksgiving of last year? Maybe? Yes, it was. They had gone to an interactive art exhibit together. Pearl had a blast, but James had been answering emails and taking calls every spare second.

Caitlin sighed, checking her texts again as if she'd missed the message she'd been waiting for half the afternoon. Still nothing. Moments like this had made her so lost about her marriage that she'd escaped to Blueberry Bay earlier in the year to visit her sister Alissa Lewis and get some perspective.

It had helped. She'd taken in the small, quiet town's charm and gotten away from the constant hustle and bustle of the restaurant and the city, gaining perspective on what she was going through. And when she'd gotten back to Denver, she had hoped that things would improve in her marriage.

James had promised he would do better at spending time with them. But so far, he was still wrapped up in the restaurant, staying late and arriving early. And when they were at home, he was attached to his laptop, sketching out plans to potentially open another restaurant. Another location to take up his time. They were able to afford it with how successful their current restaurant was, but Caitlin always pushed back against his plans when he brought them up.

And that was if they talked. Most of their conversations felt awkward, like they were on a first date where they'd run out of things to talk about over dinner but hadn't gotten the check yet. It was a far cry from the evenings they'd spent early in their marriage, talking and laughing and planning for their future.

In some ways, they had that future—their restaurant was even more successful than they had ever dreamed, they owned their own home, and they had Pearl. But it felt so much more hollow than she ever thought it would be. She was so stuck despite the bright spots, like Pearl.

Caitlin looked back to the otters, who were still floating along holding hands. An absurd rush of envy over their connection came through her and she nearly laughed. But then again, when was the last time she'd held James's hand?

All she wanted was to feel like she and Pearl were number one in his heart. That was it. But in moments like this and in little ways all the time, she felt like they were second place behind his career.

At one point, the restaurant was something for them both—their shared passion that brought them closer together. They spent hours in their kitchen, putting together ideas for the menu and making tweaks until everything was exactly as they'd envisioned. And she still loved the idea of owning a restaurant.

But now it was this weight around their marriage, something that Caitlin resented more and more every day. As if it was James's wife, not her.

"Can we see the penguins?" Pearl asked, snapping Caitlin back to attention.

"Sure, sweetheart." Caitlin took Pearl's hand. "Take me there."

They followed the big signs that had pictures of penguins on them, weaving through the crowds. The penguin area was packed too, so they stood at the back to wait their turn at the front. Pearl went on her tiptoes anyway, trying to see the penguins. Even as tall as Alissa was, she couldn't see the penguins either.

"Here, look at the sign," Caitlin said, steering Pearl toward the simple description of the penguins.

Pearl had just finished kindergarten and was already ahead in her reading, so she stopped in front of it, putting her hands on her hips. Caitlin's mouth twitched in amusement at the look of concentration on her face.

"Did you know penguins are birds? They live half their lives on land and half in the ocean. Most of them live in the southern..." she paused. "Hem..."

"Hemisphere."

"Hemisphere," Pearl continued. "But one sp-species, the... Mommy, how do I say this one?" Pearl pointed at a word.

"Galapagos," Caitlin said, enunciating each syllable.

"Galapagos penguin lives in the north." Pearl grinned, looking up at her mother.

"Amazing job!" A rush of pride replaced any negative feelings that Caitlin felt. "Your reading has gotten so good."

They worked their way to the front to see the penguins, which were diving into the enclosure's water. Caitlin loved seeing them waddling around too. After that, they went into the freshwater fish section, which they found interesting but wasn't their favorite. In Pearl's words, the fish were "very not pretty". Then they went to the tropical fish section, which they both loved more.

Pearl's excitement and happiness lifted Caitlin's mood until she checked her phone again. Still nothing from James. Pearl had been doing so well lately and was so filled with joy that Caitlin didn't want to let her know what was happening between her and her father. So far Pearl hadn't asked about where her father was since she was having so much fun, but Caitlin hoped she wouldn't.

They wove their way through their rest of the aquarium until they reached the biggest display. The room was huge, so Pearl was able to find a spot right at the glass. Caitlin jumped when her phone started to ring—James, finally. Caitlin told Pearl to stay put and kept an eye on her from a distance while she answered.

"James?" Caitlin said. "Hi, what's going on?"

Caitlin heard the chaos of the restaurant behind him. Saturdays were busy, but their staff was more than qualified to run it without them there.

"I'm still at the restaurant. Something came up that I had to take care of, so I can't make it," James said.

Caitlin closed her eyes, taking a deep breath. "What's going on?"

"Some staff didn't show and several large parties came in," he said with a sigh.

Caitlin squeezed the bridge of her nose. "Okay, but we always have the most qualified people working on Saturdays and they can handle themselves."

When Caitlin and James had talked about improving their relationship, Caitlin had pledged to give them more training, which Caitlin had found effective. Apparently James didn't feel the same way.

James didn't respond for a few moments. "It's important that I'm here."

"It's important that you spend time with your

family." Caitlin kept her voice down even though her entire body felt wound tight. "Just for an afternoon? I'm tired of you prioritizing the restaurant every single day."

"Owning a restaurant is an everyday thing, Caitlin." Caitlin could easily envision him digging his hand into his hair, pacing in the back of the kitchen. "It seems like you don't respect that."

Caitlin watched Pearl talking to another kid as they pointed to a big fish drifting past them, trying to process James's words. Of course she understood how much time it took to run a restaurant—they had started it together. But they had worked hard to get to where they were now, where their staff was good enough to operate without them breathing down their necks.

"Should we hire more help? So you don't have to be there so much?" she asked. She had brought this idea up in the past and he'd brushed her off.

"That's the thing, Caitlin. I want to be hands-on here."

Silence stretched between them, neither taking steps to break it.

"Well, then." Caitlin cleared her throat. "I'll just tell Pearl you'll see her at home."

"Okay, see you then."

He hung up and Caitlin tried to swallow the knot in her throat. Pearl looked back at her, face bright with excitement, as she pointed to a shimmering fish darting around. Her heart ached. She wished that James could see her like this, so genuinely thrilled. Was he going to miss more moments like this? Dance recitals? School events? Pearl would notice his absence more, and the thought of that broke Caitlin's heart.

Caitlin put on a smile for Pearl and came back over.

"It turns out that it's just going to be us today," Caitlin said, smoothing her hand over Pearl's head. "We'll see Daddy at home, okay?"

"Okay. Can we bring him a gift?" Pearl asked.

Caitlin's smile nearly faltered but she kept it steady. "Sure, sweetheart. That would be lovely."

CHAPTER THREE

"Careful on that ladder, Han," Willis said, passing behind her with a box of leis in his arms. He put it down on the long bar alongside the restaurant.

"I'm on the second step, Dad. I'm fine," Hannah replied, hanging up a lei on the wall of The Crab. The shop had been transformed from its usual maritime theme to a Hawaiian one to get people excited about the Blueberry Bay Luau.

"I know. But even a fall from that height would hurt." Willis picked up a foam surfboard and put it up against the wall.

Hannah suppressed a smile. Her dad was so protective sometimes.

She stepped down from her ladder and took a look around. The half of the restaurant that they'd decorated looked fun, the exact kind of energy they wanted to create. But Hannah didn't feel the same flutter of excitement in her stomach as she usually did around the luau. She had gone every year since she was little and it was one of her favorite summer events. What was different this year?

"Did you take a break?" Willis asked from behind the counter. "Did you eat lunch?"

"I did." Hannah raised her eyebrow at him, going to grab another box of Hawaiian flowers. "Did you?"

He waved her off as he walked toward the side door. "I'm fine. I need to meet the food delivery guys outside—be back in a minute."

"Okay."

Hannah folded up the ladder and carried it to the other side of the restaurant to decorate it. There was a perfect spot for some fabric hibiscus flowers along the top of the menu board, so she set up her ladder and climbed up a few steps to hang more flowers. She hated being in a low mood, especially at work where she had to have a happy face on. Most people in town knew her as bright, bubbly Hannah. But she couldn't shake it and she wasn't sure why.

The bell rang, notifying her that a customer had arrived. She looked over her shoulder—she didn't recognize the man who walked in, so he was probably a tourist. He had on glasses that were on the nerdy side of trendy, big on his attractive face. Hannah wasn't much of a beard person, but she liked his neatly trimmed one.

"Hey! I'll be with you in a moment," she said.

"Okay, no rush."

Hannah moved the ladder over so the man could see the full menu and went back behind the counter.

"What can I get you?" she asked.

"I'll take the bacon grilled cheese sandwich with chips and an iced tea, please," he said.

"Awesome." She told him the total and he handed over his card to pay. "I'll have that ready for you in a few minutes."

She went back into the kitchen and washed her hands so she could whip up the sandwich. From where she was standing, she could see through the service window. The man was wandering around as if he were looking for a place to sit, even though the place was empty at this time of day.

"Can I get anything else for you?" Hannah called, slicing some fresh bread in half.

"I was just looking for an outlet for my computer," he said.

"Ah, we only have them behind the counter." She laughed. "In all the time I've worked here, I don't think anyone's ever brought their laptop. Usually they just enjoy the view."

The man ran his hand through his hair, chuckling. "You're right. The view is amazing. My computer can wait."

"Where are you visiting from?" Hannah asked, arranging the bacon and cheese on the bread before putting on the other piece of bread and putting it under the panini press.

"Indiana. I go to business school at Indiana University, so I'm here for the summer," he said.

"Wow, nice." Hannah opened the container of chips that she and Willis had made that morning, scooping some into a red basket.

"I'm Luke, by the way," he said after a brief pause.

"I'm Hannah. It's nice to meet you," she replied. "Are you planning on doing something in particular with your degree?"

"Yeah. I want to start a tech business—fixing gadgets and electronics, mostly," he said, looking up at the decorations. He was so tall that Hannah could see him through the service window without going on her tiptoes.

"That's awesome. I'm way too scared to try to fix any electronics I break, honestly." She pulled his sandwich out of the press and sliced it in half. "I feel like I'd electrocute myself or something."

He laughed again, a broad smile on his face. His smile was the kind that brightened a room. "Yeah, that's what a lot of people say. But some things are such easy fixes. If more people got their electronics fixed instead of buying new ones every time something happened, we could reduce a lot of electronic waste in the world."

Hannah tucked his sandwich into its basket and came out with it. "Here's your sandwich. What brings you to Blueberry Bay, then? I haven't heard anything about electronics or tech around here."

"Thank you." He took the basket and picked a seat not far from the front bar. "I'm here to help my aunt and uncle with their store—Sandy and Daniel."

"Oh, I know them. Sandy's Grocery is great." Hannah rested her hands on the counter. "Sometimes I run over there if we run out of something in the back."

"Yeah, it's amazing. I'm glad to get away from campus. Sometimes it feels like I get stuck there." He bit into his sandwich, his whole demeanor brightening even more. For once, Hannah felt like a grump in comparison to someone. His positive mood boosted hers, but not by much. "This is amazing."

"Glad you like it!"

The bell above the door rang again and Hannah's breath caught in her throat. It was Michael again. He was dressed in shorts and a t-shirt, his hair tied back. She loved how it looked when it was down, but having it back emphasized his face and made him look even more sophisticated.

"Hi!" Hannah scrambled over to the register. "How are you? What can I get you?"

"Hey, I'm not bad. Just a fish sandwich, please. To go," Michael said. He was smiling broadly—was that a good sign? Was he interested in her, at least a little? It was a smile that someone gave a person they really liked, not just an acquaintance.

"Gotcha." Hannah ran him up, then went to the back to make his sandwich. While she didn't want to give him slow service, she wanted him to linger.

"The place looks nice," Michael said, standing in view of the service window. He was just as tall as Luke. "Very in the spirit of the luau."

"Thanks! We spent a long time on it." Hannah slowed down so she wouldn't cut herself while preparing the bread for Michael's sandwich.

"I can tell."

Hannah's face heated up as she tried to think of something else to say. Michael's presence scrambled her brain entirely. She finished up his sandwich and brought it out.

"Here you are," Hannah said.

"Thanks. See you next time." Michael nodded and headed out.

Hannah sighed. How was she supposed to get Michael to ask her to the luau if she could hardly string together two sentences that weren't related to taking his order? He hardly noticed her, period. She went back through that brief conversation and kicked herself for missing out so many opportunities to make herself stand out.

"You guys are going to have a booth at the luau?" Luke said.

"Yeah." Hannah messed around with a stack of cups, watching Michael's back as he disappeared around the corner.

"Cool. I'm excited. It's been a long time since I've been." Luke munched on a chip.

"Yeah," Hannah said again, all the energy to chat gone. All of her thoughts were on Michael and how she could capture his attention next.

CHAPTER FOUR

Dane Taylor leaned back in his seat, a small smile on his face. He'd just finished reading Alissa's article on the luau and as always, he was impressed. She managed to distill all of the excitement and anticipation into the article even though she had never been. He could practically feel her excitement coming through the page.

He shot back an email with his feedback on the article, then stretched, his shirt coming untucked a little. He still felt strange dressing down to some degree at work, even though he could see how much he'd loosened up in general since he started dating Alissa. He stood and tucked his shirt back in all the way. Despite Alissa's influence, he still felt a little uptight in comparison to everyone else in town in his tailored pants and shirts.

The luau was a perfect example of that. Despite Alissa's incredible article making the event sound fresh and exciting, he couldn't fully embrace the idea of something so frivolous. They were in New England. Why were they going with a Hawaiian themed event? Were people going to dress up for it? In the middle of the summer? Why was everyone going all out? He brought this up to Alissa and she laughed, squeezing his hand and telling him to not think too hard about it.

And he desperately wanted to. But his brain kept going into analysis mode. He was able to shut it off at times, but it had been locked on for the past few days. It wasn't that he didn't see any upsides. He could see several. It brought tourists to the area, which brought money to the area. That was always a good thing. But it was just a party for the sake of having a party, a concept he never fully understood. It was frustrating, to say the least.

"Hey, Dane," Josie Garner said, appearing in the doorway of his office. "I'm heading out."

"Okay, thanks for letting me know. I'll lock up." Dane couldn't keep his frustrated mood out of his voice.

Josie started to leave, but paused. "Is everything okay?"

Dane ran both of his hands through his hair. "It's just this luau. I'm just not getting it."

"It's a luau. What's there to get?" Josie asked.

"See, that's exactly it." Dane sighed. "Everyone here seems to be able to get into things like this around here and I just can't. Alissa's so enthusiastic about it and I don't want to burst her bubble."

"Is her article on it not good?"

"No, it's great. I can see why it's exciting, but I can't personally feel it within myself. That's why I'm even more confused about myself," Dane said. "I thought I'd shaken off the old me and fully embraced this town but I feel like I'm going backward. Like the other day, we saw some surfing lessons being advertised and I just couldn't bring myself to do it with her. I could tell she was a little sad about it even though she was also nervous to try it too."

His fears and anxieties started to bubble over. He was in love with Alissa, and the thought of disappointing her because of his inability to loosen up made his chest tight. Her smile made his day brighter every time and he didn't want to dim that, even a little bit. But at the same time, so many things she wanted to do made him reflexively refuse to do it, at least in his head.

Josie studied him, then leaned against the door frame.

"Well, you definitely have changed a lot lately. So you shouldn't beat yourself up about that," she said. "But Alissa has really helped you come out of your shell. Think about it. Remember that time you guys went hiking? You hadn't wanted to do that but it was a good time."

Dane did remember. He wasn't very outdoorsy. At most, he liked to walk around in a park or along the beach. But Alissa had wanted to go for a hike on a day trip, so he'd gone with her. He'd gotten a million mosquito bites, got a few gnarly blisters in his new hiking boots, and had almost fallen twice, but it really was fun to see all of the beautiful views together.

"True," Dane murmured.

"So I'm sure you'll have fun once the luau actually happens," Josie said.

"You think so?"

"I know so." Josie waved her hand, standing up straight again. "You and Alissa balance each other out perfectly. I wouldn't worry too much about not 'getting' the luau."

The knot in Dane's chest loosened a bit. He trusted Josie's word. She was great with people and always friendly, but she wasn't afraid to tell someone the truth if they needed to hear it. She wouldn't lie to him.

"Thanks, Josie," Dane said.

"No problem. See you tomorrow."

Josie left Dane to his thoughts. The heaviness in his chest had lightened, but that left him with more questions. He loved the idea and he and Alissa balanced each other out, but he wanted to show her that he was willing to keep stepping out of his comfort zone for her.

But how?

Dane grabbed a notepad and a pen—writing things long-hand always helped him when he was stuck with a problem. There were so many options for him to meet Alissa in the middle, but he wanted to find the best one.

Hannah had turned The Crab's sign from open to closed a half hour ago, but now she was finally finished wrapping things up for the day. The set of tasks that she had to do to close up the restaurant were so heavily ingrained in her that she could have done them in her sleep. Tidying, counting, sweeping, wiping down surfaces, putting the chairs up on the tables.

She took off the apron from around her waist and looked around. The restaurant was always so filled with life that seeing it empty was strange, but she welcomed the quiet today.

She wandered over to the piano that they kept in the corner of the restaurant near the entrance and sat at it, lifting the cover over the keys. It wasn't anything fancy. If she was remembering correctly, her dad had gotten it from someone who was trying to get rid of it and had it tuned up.

It had been there for ages and they kept it there for customers to mess around on it, just for fun. Sometimes people just poked around, not playing anything in particular, and others were quite good, grabbing the attention of everyone in the restaurant for a short time.

But for her, it was the place where she composed her work after hours and played her heart out without anyone around to see her. She could be completely herself.

The same piece that she had been working on for

weeks was bothering her—something about part of it didn't sound quite right, but she knew she could figure it out with enough work. She put her fingers to the keys to warm up her hands for the piano and not cooking or preparing food. The scales that she'd found online flowed easily, a good sign for tonight's playing. The repetitive motions and sounds took her mind off of the hard work of the day, all of the slightly-less-than-friendly customers and mishaps that came along with working at a restaurant floating away.

Once she was warmed up, both mentally and physically, she started on her piece. It was a melancholy song, which she usually didn't compose, but she loved it, the sticking point she had with it aside. She had it memorized, so the first minute was perfect and easy. The way the piano was facing made it hard to see the ocean outside unless she turned to look slightly behind her, but she did anyway.

Seeing the ocean at night was what had inspired the piece in the first place. It was dark and lonely, with only the moon to illuminate it. It was a sight she had seen countless times in her life, but one night it just struck her in a way it hadn't before. She had turned back and gone right to the piano, starting to play a few chords, which eventually turned into this piece.

She played up until the point she was having trouble with, then slowed, poking through the notes that she had mentally sketched out. Was it too upbeat, all of a sudden? Too thinly layered?

She sighed, going back to the beginning and trying to put herself into the mindset she was in when the song first came to her. It took her several tries to play through it again and again, but then, it clicked.

"Yes," she whispered to herself, drawing out the word as she played through the next section flawlessly. She had already thought out the ending to the song, which she played.

The satisfaction of figuring out the song's problem faded quickly into the sadness that the song evoked. What if she could nature her love for music all the time instead of at night when her fatigue of a long day on her feet made it hard to concentrate for very long?

Hannah sighed, resting her hands on her lap and looking around The Crab again. It was a large space, but the walls felt like they were closing in on her. Like the whole town was closing in on her with its familiarity, Michael aside. And he wasn't paying any attention to her anyway.

She ran her fingers along the keys from its highest notes to its lowest. Why had Luke come here of all places for the summer? From what she'd heard, Bloomington, Indiana, was a college town with a lot going on. A lot more interesting things than were here in Blueberry Bay. At least he had all of that to go back to at the end of the summer. She didn't.

A pang of guilt filled her chest. Blueberry Bay had been a great place to grow up, and The Crab was her second home. Her father had always been amazing to her, even after her mom left when she was young. She loved him, but the stagnant feeling that crept into her head every day was getting harder and harder to ignore.

CHAPTER FIVE

Caitlin pulled away from Pearl's day camp, her heart squeezing the way it always did when she left her daughter anywhere. But the thought of Pearl having fun soothed her nerves. She always talked a mile a minute about all the things she did after she came home. She never had a hard time making friends.

Caitlin pulled up her sister Alissa's phone number in her car's system and called her.

"Hey!" Alissa said when she picked up. "What's up?"

"Nothing, just wanted to say hey." Caitlin pulled into the right lane. "What's going on in Blueberry Bay?"

"It's great! So many tourists are here for the summer season. It still has that small town vibe, but

I've had to give directions at least four times this week. You'd be surprised how many people can't find the ocean despite all the views."

"Really?" A smile spread across Caitlin's face. Getting lost in the small town was hard to do. There was Main Street, which ran parallel to the boardwalk. A few other businesses branched off Main Street, but not many.

"I know. But I get it. Everyone gets turned around every once in a while."

"True. And everyone there is so friendly that it's a good place to get lost." Caitlin remembered wandering around the charming town at her own pace, stumbling upon beautiful view after beautiful view. Even in the colder weather, it was a breathtaking place.

"Definitely," Alissa said. "We're preparing for the luau too. All of the businesses are getting ready for it. It's almost like a holiday with how people are going all out. Like imagine Christmas, but instead of lights, everyone has leis and flowers and palm trees everywhere."

"That sounds like fun!"

"You'd probably love all of the food that people are planning. I've been talking to a bunch of places here and they're planning special Polynesian meals," Alissa said.

"I'd totally love that."

Caitlin had loved all of the restaurants she'd tried when she visited. She had high standards when it came to flavor—she couldn't turn off her restaurant owner brain even if she tried—but she wasn't a snob about it. She loved everything from street food to Michelin star experiences. As long as the food was good and made with care, she could appreciate it.

And there was so much to appreciate in Blueberry Bay. Even thinking about the sandwiches at The Crab made her hungry. Once she visited again, whenever that was, she was going straight there to get something.

"People are excited about all of it. Things at *The Outlet* are really picking up too, both the paper and the magazine. Our print run keeps going up and Dane has been talking to other newspaper owners in the region. News is really spreading about it, especially the magazine."

"The magazine is amazing, so I'm not at all surprised." Alissa and Dane had started it together when they realized that they could do a lot of long-form pieces on the area. "When is the next issue?"

"Not long after the luau. I'm going to write a

piece on it and it'll be the cover story." Alissa gasped in excitement. "It's going to be my best piece yet, I think, and I've only started doing some interviews. There are so many people in the area with incredible stories that haven't been told yet."

Caitlin smiled at Alissa's buckets of enthusiasm as she spoke about the people whose stories she was going to tell in the long-form article. As happy as she was for Alissa, Caitlin's heart tugged with a bittersweet feeling. She was so glad that Alissa had forged a new life for herself. She had been in such a rut at her old newspaper job. But seeing all the ways Alissa's life was branching out reminded Caitlin of how stuck she felt.

They had always been different, but the differences felt starker now. Still, nothing could dim the happiness Caitlin had for her sister.

"How have things been with you?" Alissa asked.

"Good! I just dropped Pearl off at day camp. This one is an art camp so I'm sure I'll have plenty of pieces for the fridge." Caitlin chuckled. "She's going to a theater camp in a few weeks, which should be fun for her too."

"Oh, I bet she'll love that," Alissa said. "How are things with James and the restaurant?"

The smile that had been on Caitlin's face for

most of the call faltered. She had pushed thoughts of James aside for a while, but she didn't want to keep things from her sister.

"Not great," Caitlin admitted.

"I'm sorry, Caitlin."

"Thanks. We've been trying, but nothing seems to fix the divide." Caitlin slowed to a stop at a light. "I don't know what else to do. The other day, we were supposed to go to the aquarium, but he didn't show. He called when we were most of the way through the place saying he had to stay at the restaurant."

"Oof. Did Pearl notice?"

"No, thankfully. She insisted on getting him a little gift at the gift shop." Caitlin massaged the back of her neck, thinking of the sparkly magnet they'd gotten him and put on the fridge. "Aside from that, I've tried to spend more time with him in the evenings, schedule date nights, everything. And it's just not bringing us any closer together. It's just awkward. It feels like we want completely different things at this point."

"What does he want? Out of the marriage, I mean."

"And I want to focus on us as a family. He wants to be fully devoted to the restaurant." Caitlin sighed and pulled off when the light turned green. "The restaurant is the only thing that seems to make him excited or happy these days."

"Well, you're trying, at least. What's James been doing to try to fix it?"

"We're going to couples counseling once a week."

"That's great."

Caitlin wasn't sure what to say in return. Their next appointment simultaneously felt very close and very far away. Caitlin didn't enjoy the process even if it was necessary. At first she had latched onto each appointment, hoping the counselor would reveal the key to fixing their marriage. But each time, the rift between them showed more and more.

The more James opened up about what he wanted, the more Caitlin realized that they'd started to go down different paths. Guilt squeezed in her chest until she remembered how much she had tried. And that was all she could do.

"It's a hard process," Caitlin finally said, turning off the main road to a side road she used as a shortcut to their house. "I'm not sure how I feel about it yet. We talk about our goals and keep talking past each other. The counselor is great, but it's just so hard."

"Is there anything I can do?" Alissa asked.

"No, but thank you for the support. I'm just going to keep working on it and see if things improve."

"Okay. I'm always here if you need me."

The anxiety pulsing through Caitlin slowed down. Knowing her sister was in her corner meant the world. She missed her dearly. Their time in Blueberry Bay had been one of the best times they'd ever had together. Over the years, they'd drifted apart a little bit. Alissa was flitting through life as a free spirit, making abrupt decisions that gave Caitlin heart palpitations.

Meanwhile, Caitlin was on her straight and narrow path, focused on her marriage, her business, and her daughter. She knew that she could sometimes worry about Alissa a little too much and they'd clash over their differing opinions.

But something about both of them being in a rough spot had brought them closer together, opening up about their deepest insecurities, and now they talked more than they ever had.

Maybe it was something about Blueberry Bay that brought that out in them. The town's peaceful nature brought out her contemplative side and slowing down made her understand what really mattered to her in the big scheme of things.

"I really want to visit Blueberry Bay again," Caitlin said. "It was such a nice break and I was so happy being there."

"Come any time," Alissa said. Caitlin could hear the smile in her voice. "You're always welcome."

* * *

Alissa ended her call with Caitlin and gathered her things to go into work. Today she had her usual canvas tote bag plus a big bag of luau decorations she planned to put up around the office. She'd scoured the internet to find the best ones and had spent a little bit more than she should have. But she knew it would be worth it once everything was up. Plus, the luau was an annual event and a lot of the decorations would last for years.

Instead of focusing on the decorations, her thoughts went to Caitlin. Hearing the hollow sadness in her sister's voice made Alissa's heart ache. Alissa hoped it would all get better for her. Caitlin was trying so hard to make her marriage work, but from Alissa's point of view, James wasn't putting in the same.

It made Alissa feel glad she had met Dane. They had butted heads at first—her exuberant energy against his grumpy nature -- but so far, they'd managed to work through any issues that came up. And they were on the same page about what they wanted, like the paper and magazine, as well as what they wanted their lives to look like in the future.

The conversations about the future had come together so seamlessly and she was so excited to see what the future held for them.

Alissa made her way to the office, unlocking the door since she was the first one to arrive. After putting on some fun music, she got to work.

She was glad she was tall, since it made putting up all of the decorations she'd brought a lot easier. She spent forty-five minutes stringing threads of hibiscus flowers along the wall, putting a grass skirt around the edges of everyone's desks, and putting decorative coconuts on every free surface.

Hopefully the change would get Dane hyped for the luau. So far he'd been enthusiastic about her articles on it, but he was always happy with her work. She wanted him to be excited about the actual event.

As much as she loved him, she sometimes thought he was still half-stuck in his old ways, unwilling to take a step in a new direction. He just had to let go.

"Oh, wow!" Josie stopped in the doorway of the office. "This is so festive. I love it!"

"Thanks!" Alissa straightened up the latest row of hibiscus flowers she'd hung up. "I hope it'll inspire Dane to get into the spirit of the luau."

Josie chuckled, finally coming in and shutting the door behind her.

"It's worth a shot, but you know how Dane can be sometimes." Josie put her bag down next to her desk and sat at her computer.

"True." Alissa studied Josie for a moment. Something was different about the newspaper's secretary, but she couldn't pinpoint what. "Is that dress new? It's really pretty."

"It is, thank you!" Josie beamed. "I just got it from that boutique in town. The new one off Main."

Josie had noticed the boutique before on her strolls through town, but she hadn't gone in. Her style was all about being comfortable and casual. Today she had gone with her favorite linen pants and an oversized button-down shirt, also made of linen, to combat the heat.

Josie's summer outfits were always as pretty as she was—dresses, printed skirts, fashionable blouses. Alissa could easily imagine her in the city in law school, where she had been before she moved to

Blueberry Bay. A law career wasn't for her, so she had come to town and hadn't looked back. Without her, the paper wouldn't have been as successful as it was. She never missed all of the small details that made the paper great.

Alissa put up a few more decorations, then went to her office. She and Josie got along well, but she wondered if Josie and Dane would have pictured themselves together. They were both from big city backgrounds and Josie balanced out Dane's brusque tendencies with kind professionalism. Plus, both of them were very good-looking. Alissa was happy with her looks, but she couldn't deny that Josie was pretty too.

A nervous pit grew in Alissa's stomach, but she downed her iced coffee to get rid of it. They had known each other for a long time and hadn't indicated that their feelings were any more than friendly. Dane loved her and showed her every day in big and small ways. She had nothing to worry about.

But still, Alissa wondered when someone was going to sweep Josie off her feet.

* * *

Luke had quickly acclimated to working at Sandy's Grocery. The experience of being there was so different than the stores back in Indiana. It was easier to get a sense of everything that the store had to offer since it wasn't a sprawling mega-store like he shopped at back in Indiana, and he saw the same people over and over again.

He'd started to remember their names and what they usually purchased too. It was satisfying to make someone's day with something as simple as the right brand of soap or oatmeal raisin cookies. He knew the feeling. As silly as it sounded, sometimes finding the perfect melon or a sponge that cut dishwashing time down by half was enough to make his day.

"I'm glad you guys have this cheese again," a stylishly dressed woman said as she dumped an armful of packaged brie from a local farm onto the counter. "It's worth the walk over from Whale Harbor."

Luke smiled and scanned the cheese, which was encased in classy packaging. "It must be good. I should try it."

"It's a guest favorite. With some fresh bread and a glass of wine?" The woman sighed dreamily as she handed Luke her card. "Perfect."

"A guest favorite?" Luke inserted her card into the chip reader.

"Yes, I own a B&B called Literary Stays not too far from here." She pushed her brightly colored glasses up on her nose.

"Ah okay. I'm new here so I'm still getting a good lay of the land. I came around when I was younger, but it's been a while," Luke said. "At least for the summer. Sandy and Daniel are my aunt and uncle."

"Ah, so you're Luke! Sandy mentioned you the other week. I'm Monica Watson." She extended her hand and Luke shook it.

"Nice to meet you."

"Nice to meet you as well." Monica smiled. "Welcome to Blueberry Bay."

"Thanks for the welcome! I'll have to check out Whale Harbor sometime." Luke bagged up all the cheese. "And maybe try some of this cheese with bread and wine. I don't know a thing about wine, though."

"A good chardonnay or a pinot noir would be fabulous. Yves over at Blueberry Bay Wines will give you a perfect recommendation every time."

"Great, I'll have to stop by." He held the bag up to Monica so she could easily grab the handle. "Enjoy."

"Thanks!"

Monica left, finishing off the short line that had been at the register. She was far from the first person to welcome him to town. It seemed like Sandy and Daniel knew every single person in town and had told them about Luke's arrival. Everyone had made him feel right at home and were more than happy to offer recommendations to make his time here even better.

"Hey, Sandy?" Luke said to Sandy, who was messing with the computer at the far end of the long register. "I have a free moment to look at the computer."

"Oh, perfect!" Sandy let out a sigh of relief. "I don't know what happened. At first I thought the problem was because we dropped the laptop, but it seems like it's an issue with every computer that has the inventory software."

Luke took Sandy's spot at the computer. "What's happening?"

"Whenever I try to add a new product, it works, but when I try to update the number of the inventory above ten, it resets." Sandy sighed, running her fingers through the end of her ponytail. "But that only happens some of the time."

"Did you turn the computer off and on?" Luke asked.

"Yep." The corner of Sandy's mouth quirked up. "I'm not tech-savvy, but I've got that part down."

Luke grinned. "Just had to check. I'll see what I can do."

Luke dove into the problem. The software was old school and probably needed to be ditched in favor of something new, but he wasn't going to bring that up yet. Sometimes an issue just needed a few small tweaks to be fixed.

As he always did, he got sucked into the problem, trying new angles and thinking about what the answers could possibly be. Customers came in and out, only stealing his attention for a fraction of a second. But then, Hannah came in.

She was wearing a t-shirt with The Crab's logo on it and denim shorts, her jet black hair up in a bun. His cheeks flushed even though she hadn't looked at him yet. He couldn't deny his interest in her. She was cute and seemed really nice.

If he were back in Indiana, he might have had a chance. But Hannah's interest in Michael, who had come into the store and introduced himself the other day, was clear. The moment Michael walked in, Luke faded into the background. Luke didn't blame her. Any woman would have had a crush on a man like that.

"Hey, Hannah," Sandy said with a smile. "Do you need any help today?"

"Hey, Sandy! I'm just here to pick up some things for The Crab," Hannah said.

"Ah, right, Daniel put together your order in the back. Let me grab it." Sandy slipped past Luke to go to the back, leaving Hannah and Luke alone.

"Hi." Luke waved. "How are you?"

"Not bad." Hannah wandered over toward him, her hands tucked into her back pockets. "Just a regular summer day. Things are pretty crazy over at The Crab. We almost ran out of some things, so I had to come here to pick them up."

"I'm not surprised that you're busy. The food is so good."

"Thanks." Hannah smiled, glancing at the computer. "What are you up to?"

"Just trying to fix the computer. It's probably just a software issue since the problem is happening on more than one computer, but the way the fans are going on this thing makes me think everything might be an issue." He pointed downward, where the main part of the computer was. "It sounds like it's about to take off like a rocket, at least from where I'm standing."

Hannah snorted, leaning in. "Ah, now I hear it. Yeah, that does sound pretty bad."

"It should be an easy fix if it's something with the computer itself." Luke gripped the edge of the counter so he wouldn't scratch at his beard, a nervous habit of his. "I just have to open it up and take a look at some things."

"How did you learn how to fix things?" Hannah asked, tilting her head to the side and studying him in a way that made his face heat even more.

"A lot of trial and error. And electronics taken apart, to my parents' chagrin." Luke shrugged. "Luckily people in my neighborhood growing up loved yard sales, so I picked up old stuff and starting figuring out how it works. Technology has seriously advanced, but I've found a method to figure things out."

"That's really cool." Hannah sounded genuinely impressed, making Luke's chest expand with pride.

"We're really lucky to have Luke here for all of our tech issues," Sandy said, returning from the back weighed down by several paper bags. "If only for the summer. Blueberry Bay doesn't have a tech genius on demand."

"Blueberry Bay doesn't have a lot of things," Hannah said, her tone abruptly dry. "Thanks for this, Sandy."

"No problem, hun. See you around."

"See you. Bye, Luke." Hannah gave him a half smile and left.

Luke pushed down his disappointment that she'd left so soon and went back to fixing the computer.

CHAPTER SIX

Dane came home to the scent of something delicious wafting from the house. He smiled—Alissa had a key and had told him not to pick up any dinner since she had it covered. Coming home to little surprises like this was one of the many reasons why he loved her. Sometimes she surprised him with something she baked and he returned the favor by surprising her with a book. He'd never been with someone who made such an effort to make him feel good.

He unlocked the door and the sound of hula music floated to his ears.

"Alissa?" he called, kicking off his shoes next to the door.

"The kitchen!"

He followed the sound and the smells of Alissa's

famous (to him) creamy chicken, finding her where she said she'd be. But instead of cooking, she was dancing, swaying her hips to the music with a huge grin on her face. Her smile always filled his chest with butterflies, even though they'd been together for a while now.

"Hey!" Alissa danced toward him, extending her hand. "Dance with me."

Dane rubbed the back of his neck, which was quickly heating. Just the thought of dancing made him feel uncomfortable in his skin. "I don't dance."

"Come on, not even a little?" Alissa danced around him, resting her hands on his shoulders as she passed behind him. "Not even a little head bob?"

"Not even. Trust me. I don't want to hurt your eyes." Dane kissed her forehead when she came around his front again.

"Oh, fine." Alissa squeezed both of his arms. "The food will be ready in a second."

"Okay. Let me change and I'll be right back."

Dane changed out of his tailored dress shirt and slacks into sweatpants and a t-shirt, something he'd never wear out in public. When he returned to the kitchen, Alissa had set the small table over in his breakfast nook.

"I got this white wine. I have no idea if it'll be

good or not, but the person at the store said that it would go well with the chicken," Alissa said, squinting at the wine bottle's label for a moment before attempting to open it. After failing to pop the cork, she smiled sheepishly and extended it toward Dane.

Dane took the bottle and corkscrew, popping it open with ease and filling her glass, then his. They sat down at the table together, their knees brushing together.

Dane took a bite of the chicken and potatoes, making sure to get plenty of the rich, creamy sauce. The flavor exploded on his tongue. Alissa might not have had a lot of recipes up her sleeve, but the ones she had were amazing. The wine was a perfect complement.

"This is amazing every single time," Dane said.

"Thank you! I'm glad you still love it." Alissa smiled. "I figured you'd be tired of it by now."

"I don't think I could ever be tired of it."

They dug in more earnestly. It had been a long day and they were both hungry.

"What did you think about my article on the luau?" Alissa asked once they had eaten more.

"It was some of the best work you've ever done," Dane said without missing a beat.

It truly was. He was always amazed by her ability to capture the energy of something she had never been to before. But she had outdone herself this time. She had found the perfect people to interview and brought their stories to life. He couldn't wait until after the luau when she would get to write a long-form piece about it for the magazine. That was where her writing skills really shined. She blended her ability to tell an incredible story with her talent for research, creating pieces that he was proud to be the editor of.

Alissa beamed behind her wine glass.

"Yeah?" she asked.

"Of course. I think everyone is going to love it," Dane said.

"Great! I'm so excited about the luau. The next promo article should be even better. I'm going to talk to someone who's made leis for the event for the past five years. She moved here with her husband from Hawaii." Alissa cut into her chicken and took a bite. Dane waited for her to swallow since he could tell she was bursting to finish her point. "And I'm going to try to talk to as many vendors as possible since they're bringing so much business to town. Plus, they make it fun. It'll be great for the community."

Dane smiled, but he couldn't bring the same

energy to it as Alissa could. It all *sounded* great—more business in town meant more attention on the paper and magazine, and that meant that both could grow. He could easily get excited about that.

But it wasn't hitting him as deeply as he felt it should have, even after loving Alissa's article. Alissa's enthusiasm usually leaked over to him, whether it was about a dog they passed on their regular walks or a new sandwich at The Crab. For whatever reason this luau wasn't the same.

Was it because it was a big event? Something social where there was a risk he'd feel out of place? He wasn't sure. But he wished he could shake the feeling with a little logical thinking.

Maybe that was the crux of the issue—he was out of his element, so he needed some confidence to get him out of his shell. But getting that confidence was the hard part.

He sipped his wine. Then an idea hit him, and a flare of excitement bubbled up in his chest.

* * *

Hannah hauled her surfboard toward the water, tugging up the zipper of her wetsuit. Her dad had told her that she could start work late today, so she figured she'd go out and catch a few waves before her shift at The Crab.

It was a gorgeous day. The sun was bright and warm, a nice contrast to water that still hadn't fully warmed up from the winter. A lot of other surfers were taking advantage of the perfect conditions, catching waves in groups or alone.

She paddled out onto the water. It felt like it had been ages since she had been out on the water, but her muscle memory took over. Her first few waves were small and easy, just to get herself back into the motion of balancing on the board, feeling the ocean underneath her.

She missed being out on the water like this. So much of her time was spent at The Crab, helping her dad run it day to day and getting into the business end of things when he had a moment to teach her. And she spent her evenings at the piano, not that she could get out on the water then. Getting fresh air, and not just from delivering orders on the patio of The Crab, was making her feel alive again.

She spotted the perfect wave off in the distance and she prepared to hop up on her board.

She caught it right on time, but it was much, much bigger than she anticipated. She wobbled, but caught her balance again, skimming across the wave.

Her board caught a slight swell that sent her flying off into the wave beneath her.

The shock of the cold water surrounding her body so suddenly knocked the breath out of her, making her panic. She thrashed around, trying to figure out which was way up. Her swimming skills were strong, but that was when she was calm. Now she wasn't sure if she could fight her way back to the surface.

When her head came above water for a moment, she gasped for air, the salt water stinging her eyes. Relief filled her, even as she coughed, but it was short lived.

Another wave crashed over her head and she dipped under the water again. This time, she knew which way was up, so she kicked up to the surface, trying to grab her board. It was attached to her ankle, so it hadn't floated away, to her relief, but grabbing it and hauling her body halfway on it was difficult

She coughed once she got her head out of the water, sputtering and trying to get her bearings. When she finally managed to stay above water for more than a second, she was ridiculously far from shore.

She tried her best to not panic, but it was hard not to in a situation like this. Everyone looked miniature, as if she were looking at a doll's house. And the combination of her panic and the effort it had taken to swim back to the surface made her limbs feel heavy and tired. How was she going to make it back to shore? What if the waves kept carrying her farther and farther away from shore?

Tears pricked her eyes and her chest ached. Her board was keeping her afloat, but for how long? What if she drowned from her fatigue? She wasn't usually afraid of the open ocean, but being at this distance made her hyperaware of all the sea creatures passing underneath her in the dark water. It was completely irrational to fear getting attacked by a shark, but the fear still settled in her head.

Hannah didn't like feeling hopeless, but all of this was driving that feeling home. How was she going to get back?

But thankfully, someone paddled next to her, steadying her board. It was Michael, straddling his board.

"You okay?" Michael asked. "That was quite the wave."

"Um, yes. I'm just..." Hannah sputtered again, her cheeks going hot. Of course he saw her wipe out. But then again, he came up to her like a knight in shining armor to help. That had to mean something. "I'm just pretty far from shore."

"I'll help you get back."

As Michael guided her back to shore, Hannah's heart pounded for reasons besides that accident. Was Michael worried about her because he saw her differently than before? She glanced up at him. His long, dark hair was wet and down around his broad shoulders, which she usually only saw when he came into The Crab directly after coming off the water. It looked good on him.

They finally made it back to shore, and Michael picked up her board for her, carrying both.

"I-I've got it," Hannah said, stumbling on the sand. Her legs were much more wobbly from the incident than she expected. She coughed again, her mouth tasting salty.

"It's okay. You're shaken up." Michael smiled. "Focus on getting your land legs back. Sit down for a second."

Michael's smile nearly sent Hannah off kilter again. Instead, she sat down in the sand so quickly that she felt woozy. To her surprise, Michael sat down too. He wasn't overly close, but his proximity was enough for Hannah to feel too wound up to settle down. She savored his presence. Was being this close to him making it harder for her to get her head back on straight after the fall? She had no idea if she should say something.

"Thank you for your help," she finally said.

"It's seriously no problem. I've been there," he replied. "Once when I was a teenager, I went too far out to catch a good wave and got swept out farther from shore. It took me ages to get back and when I got back on the beach I just laid there for a few moments. I wasn't like you though—I was being a dumb, cocky teenager who thought he could do anything. You just got swept up with some tough waves."

Hannah tried to imagine Michael as a teenaged boy, gangly and headstrong, but couldn't. He had the lean, strong body of a surfer and always exuded confidence, not cockiness. But she remembered how the boys she went to high school with were versus how they were now, not even that long after they graduated. There was a world of difference.

"That makes me feel better," Hannah said. "It's hard to imagine you struggling out there."

Michael shrugged. "The pros are often the ones who have fallen the most. We just get a little more graceful with it."

The slight smile on Michael's face made

Hannah's heart flip in her chest again. As much as she wanted to stay there and soak in his presence, she knew she had to go.

"I should go." Hannah made her way to her feet and Michael did as well.

He walked alongside her toward the boardwalk, stabilizing her when she slipped on the sand.

Thankfully, they reached the boardwalk so she wouldn't make yet another mistake.

"Where are you headed?" Michael asked.

"The Crab. I dropped most of my stuff off there."

"Okay, let's go." He picked up the boards again and headed that way.

"You don't have to walk me," Hannah said, mentally kicking herself after. On one hand, she didn't want to take him away from the waves for too long. But on the other, he was walking her home and he didn't have to after sitting next to her to make sure she was okay. That was meaningful.

The walk to The Crab wasn't long, and soon they were walking through the front door. Willis was at the front register, wiping down the counter. He looked up at them, alarm in his eyes.

"You okay?" Willis asked, putting his rag down and coming around the counter.

"I'm fine." Hannah brushed her fingers through

her damp hair, getting caught on a knot. "Michael helped me."

"Yeah. I saw Hannah out on a wave that was unexpectedly difficult and saw her fall. I came over to see if she was okay and helped her back to shore."

Willis ran a hand through his graying hair, worry creasing his forehead. "You're completely okay, Hannah?"

"Yeah, just a little shaken up, but fine. The water was super cold." Hannah tried to smile. She was still more shaken up than she anticipated, even after sitting down for a while.

"Thank you, Michael," Willis said.

"It's not a problem at all." Michael smiled, adjusting his board in his arms. "I'd help anyone out after a fall like that."

Hannah's heart sank. He'd help anyone out? Michael was a nice person, so she shouldn't have been surprised. She doubted that he'd say that if he saw her as anyone besides Hannah, the girl who worked at The Crab.

But then again, he'd taken time out of his schedule to make sure she was okay, way more time than he had to. He ran a business and was a pro surfer with sponsorships—his schedule was probably packed.

Hannah tried to untangle her hair again, even though it frustrated her more than she already was. What did all of this mean? She felt like he'd finally noticed her, but was he noticing her in the way she wanted to be seen? She wished she could see into his head and understand where he was coming from so she wouldn't drive herself crazy trying to figure it out.

"I've got to get going," Michael said. "Take care."

"Thanks again," Hannah said softly as Michael left.

"You're sure you're okay?" Willis asked, studying Hannah for cuts and bruises. "You should go home and rest of the day."

"I'm fine, Dad. I promise." Hannah took her board toward the back. "I can work my shift."

Besides, she needed a distraction from her disappointment, and juggling everything that came with a day at the restaurant.

CHAPTER SEVEN

"Wow, really?" Sandy said to Daniel as they walked through the store. Luke perked his ears up. The two of them knew a lot about everything that was going on in town, and he couldn't help but be curious. Something about Sandy's tone told him it was very important.

"Yeah. She hit a rough wave and went tumbling off, super far out from the shore. She was lucky that Michael was out there. It could have been so much worse," Daniel said.

"What happened?" Luke asked, peering his head around the end cap of a shelf.

"Hannah Jenkins took a spill when she was out in the water. Apparently it just happened this morning," Sandy said.

Luke's heart leapt into his throat. He didn't know much about surfing around here, but falling off your board in the middle of the ocean sounded terrifying no matter where you were.

"Is she okay?" Luke asked.

"Yeah, just shaken up. Or so I heard," Daniel said with a shrug. "You know how things can be here. The actual truth of the situation gets a little bent as it travels."

"Oh. Maybe I could swing by The Crab a little before my shift ends?" He ran his hand through his hair. "Just to see if she's really okay, I mean."

Nothing got past Sandy. She gave him a sly smile that made his cheeks go hot. Was he that transparent about his crush on her? He hoped not. Sandy knew him better than most, but he feared everyone else in town knew about his feelings.

"Of course it's all right," Sandy said.

"Thanks."

Luke finished up his work and left, walking over to The Crab. He pushed his hair out of his face, hoping it was lying flat. Luckily he was just wearing a t-shirt and jeans, which he would have worn anyway.

When he walked into The Crab, he saw Hannah delivering baskets of sandwiches to clusters of people around the shop. She moved with practiced ease through the tables, though she looked even paler than usual.

"Hey," Hannah said when she noticed him.

"Hey."

"What can I get you?" Hannah asked, slipping back behind the counter.

He hadn't thought this through. "A soda would be great."

Hannah laughed half-heartedly. "They sell soda at the store, you know. There's a whole aisle of the stuff."

"Okay, true." He smiled. "But it doesn't have fountain soda."

"You have a point. Sometimes it's extra good and bubbly."

"Yeah. Actually, I came over to check on you. Sandy and Daniel said you had an accident on the water," he said.

Hannah rolled her eyes. "Wow, word travels fast around here."

Her attitude didn't faze him. "It does. Are you all right?"

"I'm fine," Hannah snapped, yanking a cup off the stack next to the fountain machine. "Of course I am. It was just a fall. It's surfing—it happens."

Luke noticed the tears gathered at the corners of her eyes, threatening to spill over.

"Here, let's take a second," Luke said softly, going behind the counter. "Is there a place to sit in the back?"

For a moment he worried that Hannah wasn't going to do it, that she'd suck it up and move through her day despite the burden on her shoulders. But her posture slumped and she nodded.

"Yeah, outside if you don't mind sitting on a crate." She sniffed, dabbing at her eyes with the back of her hand.

She led him outside and he rested his hand on her shoulder. Once they sat down, he pulled her into a quick hug. She still smelled like the sea, salty and fresh, and leaned against him for a solid second.

"It must have been scary for you," Luke said, letting his hand fall back into his lap.

"It was. I thought I was going to drown or run out of energy while trying to swim back to shore." She sniffed and let out a shuddering breath. "The water just came over me so fast. I've been surfing so many times and nothing like that has ever happened to me. And then I was so panicked that I just became even more irrational and started worrying about being eaten by a shark or something. "

A tear fell over her cheek and she wiped it away.

"And... then..." She paused, pulling herself together. "I mean, I'm grateful that Michael saved me. It would be stupid not to be grateful. But... I don't know."

He waited for her to gather her thoughts.

"I mean, I thought it might mean something, you know?" She sighed and looked up at the sky. "But it didn't. I think he was just being nice. I don't know. I really am shaken, I guess."

"I don't blame you," Luke said, even as his heart deflated.

She had gotten into an accident that could have seriously injured her and she was worried about what Michael thought. Luke didn't find that silly, of course. It just showed that she had serious feelings for the pro surfer. He had feelings that were just as intense. Namely for her.

Luke wasn't sure how to address that, or if he even should. He felt something for Hannah, a crush, maybe, but his feelings weren't important. She had gone through something terrifying. So instead, he focused on the real issue at hand: how she felt.

He let her gather herself, the slow trickle of tears coming from her eyes coming to a stop.

"I'm grateful that you're okay," Luke said once

she was more or less back to normal. "Just let me know if there's anything I can do, okay?"

Hannah finally smiled at him, though it was watery.

"Thanks, Luke. I really appreciate your kindness and concern," she said. "It means a lot."

"It's no problem at all."

"I should get back to work." Hannah stood and so did Luke. "See you around."

"See you."

Luke headed out without his soda, giving Hannah one more glance over his shoulder before he left.

CHAPTER EIGHT

"Have fun, sweetheart!" Caitlin said to Pearl, planting a kiss on her forehead.

"Bye!" Pearl rushed off to be with her friends, hardly giving Caitlin a second glance. Caitlin smiled —she was so glad that the days of Pearl crying when she got dropped off at daycare were over, though leaving her daughter still pulled at her heartstrings. She was growing up so fast, as cliché as it sounded.

Caitlin hopped back into her car and drove off toward the restaurant, taking a deep breath and letting it out. She usually did some work at home before going in, but today she wanted to go in early to meet him in the middle. The restaurant really did take a lot of work, so she thought that coming in with him in the morning to work together would be a great start.

She absently ran her hands down her steering wheel. Back when they first started the restaurant, they'd spent the early morning hours together in the kitchen, trying to get everything done themselves. Even though it had been so stressful and they had worked late into the night, it had been fun. They were in it together.

Maybe if they found that kind of spark again, he'd feel that their one restaurant would be enough and that they didn't have to expand for him to be happy.

After she swung into the nearby coffee shop to get lattes for them both, she drove to the restaurant and parked in her spot on the side of the building. The usual noise of the kitchen washed over her when she pushed open the kitchen door. Their kitchen staff were knee-deep in preparing for the day, chopping ingredients and starting the dishes that had a long cook time.

"Morning!" Caitlin said with a smile, making her way toward the office off the hallway.

She turned the corner and stopped. From where she was standing, she could see inside the open door of the office. James was talking with one of their suppliers, April. She was a beautiful woman, someone Caitlin had spoken with before and seen James speak with before.

But something about the way they were talking struck her as odd. Had they ever stood so close together as they talked? It felt like they were very close, smiling and laughing as if they were sharing a joke. The way James was laughing and smiling brought out the lines that fanned out around his eyes, the one that she had always liked. She hadn't seen them in ages.

And she didn't know April as well, but she could tell that she was looking at James as if he were something special. Like she liked him more than she should have.

Caitlin went back around the corner, her back to the wall. A knot formed in her throat. They hadn't seen her because their conversation went on as it had before.

She was well aware of the problems in her marriage, but she never thought James would cheat on her. Now she wasn't sure. The door was open, yes, but the way they were looking at each other...

She closed her eyes for a moment and regained

her composure. Had things gotten so bad that James would have an affair? Had she been missing something all along?

* * *

Alissa savored the blast of cold air that washed over her as she stepped into *The Outlet*'s offices. The midday heat had made her sweat in her short walk during her lunch break, even in her light, loose linen dress. Blueberry Bay captured both ends of the temperature spectrum, to her chagrin. She made a mental note to take a walk on the boardwalk later, just to get the cool breeze coming off the ocean.

To her surprise, Josie wasn't there to greet her as she usually was. Alissa shrugged and went back to her office. Right after she settled in, Dane knocked on the door frame to her office.

"Hey," Dane said, tucking a hand into the pocket of his pants. "I'm about to head out. Josie and I are having a business meeting over lunch at The Crab."

"Oh." Alissa hardly kept the surprise out of her voice, but Dane didn't seem to notice. Of course, Dane and Josie had had business meetings before, but they hadn't had one without her since she started working for *The Outlet*. But this time, it bothered her. Why wasn't she being included? What could they possibly be talking about that she couldn't overhear?

Still, Alissa forced a smile onto her face. "Okay. Have a good lunch," she said. "I'll keep an eye on the front desk while you guys are out."

"Thanks, Alissa." Dane came into the office and gave her a quick kiss on the lips. "See you in a bit."

Dane left and Alissa tried to turn her attention back to her work. But every time she put her fingers to the keyboard, her mind drifted to where Josie and Dane were. Alone, together.

Why was it bothering her so much? Dane had never shown interest in Josie, ever, and he had known her longer than he had known Alissa. Surely the meeting was nothing. Something to do directly with Josie's role. It was probably nothing.

Alissa turned her attention to her work and got some words down in between answering emails before more worries came floating through her head. Why hadn't Dane asked her to the luau yet? They were dating and they discussed the luau almost every day at this point, so it was a given that they'd go together.

But still. She wanted to be asked. What was he waiting for? Did he even want to go with her?

She sighed, tugging at one of her curls and trying to focus on her writing.

* * *

Hannah yawned, rounding the corner to Tidal Wave Coffee. It was the middle of the afternoon, but she desperately needed a pick-me-up before the dinner shift at The Crab. The dinner rush was something else during the summer. Customer after customer with barely a second to breathe in between. A coffee was her last line of defense.

She pushed the door open, making the bell above it jingle. In her slight brain fog, she was entirely unprepared to see Michael standing behind the counter, running the shop. Her face heated up immediately. How did he make a simple dark blue t-shirt and apron look so cool? He had his hair tied back today, a lock of it falling onto his forehead.

She realized she was standing there in the doorway, gaping, and walked in.

"Hey, Michael," Hannah said. "I didn't expect to see you behind the counter today."

"Hey!" Michael smiled. "Yeah, one of my

employees who was supposed to be on shift called out sick so I'm filling in. What can I get you today?"

"A large coffee with oat milk and extra sugar, please."

"Gotcha." Michael rang her up, then grabbed a big cup from the stack next to him. "Dark roast or light roast?"

"Dark roast."

He turned and filled up her cup with dark roast, then reached under the counter to the fridge to get the oat milk.

"You came in at just the right time," Michael said, adding oat milk to her cup. "It's been busy today but there's finally been a lull. Tuesdays are definitely an afternoon coffee kind of day. Makes me appreciate my employees even more."

"Yeah, they're all great," Hannah said. She fidgeted with the strap of her bag, trying to think of something else to say. Being around him was getting easier, but looking at him for too long still made her tongue-tied.

Michael put the oat milk back, then handed her the cup and the squeeze bottle of simple syrup. Hannah liberally squeezed the liquid sugar into her cup, then tasted it before adding a few more squirts.

"Do you always get oat milk?" Michael asked.

"Um, most of the time. It's nice. Why?"

Was he trying to memorize her order? Hannah's heart raced as if she'd already chugged her whole cup.

"I'm putting together some new drinks and oat milk seems popular." Michael shrugged and Hannah's heart slowed down. "Anyway, how are you feeling?"

"Fine." Hannah's cheeks reddened. "I still feel silly that you had to come out there and save me."

"It's no trouble at all, Hannah." Michael took the simple syrup back once Hannah finished with it. "I really didn't mind."

Hannah wasn't sure what to say in response. Did he mean that he was happy to save her in particular? The smile on his face suggested it. Maybe. Hannah wasn't entirely sure, but she was more optimistic that he meant more than he said he did this time. If he had just saved her without thinking of her as more than just Hannah, the nice girl who worked at The Crab, he wouldn't have asked about how she was again. Right?

Her heart fluttered, more out of excitement than nerves this time. Riding the wave of courage that this realization brought her, Hannah cleared her throat and said, "Are you looking forward to the Blueberry Bay Luau?"

"Yeah, of course." He smiled again, deepening the faint smile lines that fanned out around his eyes. "I'm always up for all the surfing and the food. Are you excited?"

"For sure. The Crab is going to have a lot of great food, so I'll be working a lot, but I have some time off." She bit her bottom lip for a moment, calling on the last pieces of courage that she needed. "A lot of people are asking each other so they have someone to dance with during the event."

Sure, she wasn't asking him to the luau directly, but she felt like she had put the idea out there for him to think about.

"Yeah, I heard that." His smile broadened. "I'm sure it'll be fun for everyone, even if they can't dance."

The bell above the door jingled again, and Michael looked past her at the next customers. Hannah turned too, catching sight of a group of three people entering the shop. They looked like out-of-towners, and from experience, she knew tourists expected faster service than the locals

"I've got to get going to The Crab," Hannah said. "I'll see you around."

"See you."

Hannah left, turning over her interaction with Michael in her head again and again. Maybe she didn't have to wait for him to ask her. Maybe, if he showed her a little interest, she could ask him to the luau instead.

CHAPTER NINE

Dane ran both of his hands through his hair and sighed, glancing at the how-to video on hula dancing that Josie had pulled up on the screen of her computer again. The person giving the tutorial made it look so easy, but whenever he tried, he felt like a baby horse trying to take its first step. Except he wasn't getting to the stage where he could take off and run.

Trying to learn how to do this in the office after hours was even more awkward. Usually the office was the place where he felt the most in control, the most competent. Now he felt anything but. Was asking Josie to help him learn how to hula dance a bad idea?

"Can we go back a little?" Dane asked. "Maybe about five seconds?"

"Sure." Josie rewound the video and pressed play again. Just seeing the person demonstrate on the video made Dane feel embarrassed all over again. "Are you okay?"

"I'm... fine, I guess." Dane rested his hands on his hips.

"It's okay to be a little embarrassed when you're learning something new," Josie said.

"I'm way beyond a little embarrassed." Dane snorted. "I feel like I have two left feet, and they're both backward too."

Josie laughed. "You're not *that* bad."

"But I am pretty bad."

Josie tugged at her ponytail. "You're learning. That's not the same thing as being bad at something."

She had a point, Dane supposed. He was just so out of his depth that he didn't know how to gauge his own progress.

"And don't forget how happy Alissa will be when you finally show her your moves. She'll be so surprised," Josie added.

"True." Dane took a deep breath and let it out. He had to keep that in mind. This was all for her. "Let's try it again."

Josie pressed play on the video again, copying the moves with ease. The dance classes she said she had taken as a kid and in high school were still coming in handy. Dane tried to mirror her movements, but each of his feet seemed to be controlled by a different person. And his arms were on another planet entirely. He and Josie burst out laughing.

"Okay, let's slow down," Josie said, hitting pause on the video. "Maybe this video is too advanced."

"The title of the video is literally 'hula dancing for absolute beginners.'"

"Well, maybe it's the video and not you." Josie clicked onto another one. "I think the issue is that you're trying to do your hands and your feet at the same time and it's tripping you up. Let's try just the feet first."

Josie stood next to Dane and coached him through where to put his feet and how to move his hips.

"Okay, I think you've got it," Josie said, stepping back to the computer. "Let's try it to the music."

She hit play on the video and Dane started the dance using just his feet. Splitting his upper and lower halves helped immensely. He still felt awkward, definitely, but he was able to follow the short tutorial.

"There we go!" Josie said once he ran through it twice. "You're getting there."

"Yeah?" Dane asked.

"Definitely."

Dane half-smiled. "Good. I still feel goofy, though. I can't remember the last time I moved like this."

"It'll be worth it in the end." Josie went back to the beginning of the video. "I promise."

"I hope so." Dane shook out his legs. "Let's do it again."

* * *

Alissa sat down at her desk, her stomach pleasantly full after her lunch. She was glad she had gone for a salad with chicken, strawberries, and a lemon poppyseed dressing. It was light, but filling enough to last her for a while.

She went to wake her computer up and noticed a folded note with her name on it next to the mouse pad, written in Dane's familiar blocky handwriting.

Her heart skipped a beat. Was he asking her to the luau?

She opened the note and her heart sank as she read it. He had been in and out all morning, so the note just said how much he missed and loved her. She sighed, folding it back up and putting it down in front of her. It was sweet and she appreciated it, but she couldn't shake the disappointment that it wasn't what she thought it would be.

The luau was coming up quickly. Did he not want to ask her? Did he not want to go? He told her how excited he was about her work, so she assumed so. Maybe she was wrong. Or worse, maybe she was missing something. He had been a little bit secretive lately, working late some days without going into what he was working on. Maybe it had something to do with the financial side of the paper, which she wasn't as privy to.

She tucked the note in her desk, where she kept other notes Dane had left her, and blew a curl out of her line of vision. At first she thought she was worrying for no reason, but the longer this went on, the more questions she had.

Before she could ruminate any longer, the door to the office opened. Since Josie was out to lunch, Alissa went to greet whoever it was.

"Oh, hey, Hannah," Alissa said with a smile. "What's up?"

"Hey!" Hannah held up a folded piece of paper. "I just came to drop off The Crab's specials for the luau. I was in the area and figured I'd drop off the hard copy."

"Perfect, thank you!" Alissa took the paper from her and unfolded it. She wanted to print it in the paper ahead of time to get people excited. "Oh, this all sounds amazing!"

The menu was varied, a mix of New England classics like lobster rolls and Hawaiian-inspired flavors. Alissa couldn't wait to try them all.

"I think so too! Dad and I worked hard on it," Hannah said. "But I'm super nervous about actually pulling it off. We're going to have all hands on deck but there are a lot of moving parts."

"I'm sure it'll be great. You guys haven't disappointed at any events I've been to." Alissa closed the folded menu.

"Thanks." Hannah hesitated, pulling at the end of her long, dark braid. "I hope you're right."

Hannah was usually upbeat, so seeing her so nervous threw Alissa off. It had to be more than just the menu for the luau.

"Is everything okay?" Alissa asked. "Or is it just the menu for the luau that's bothering you?"

Hannah shifted her stance, a half-smile coming

onto her face. "Is it that obvious?"

"Well, usually you don't get this nervous over The Crab." Alissa perched on the edge of Josie's desk. "So I figured I'd ask."

"It's kind of silly." Hannah shrugged. "It's just about this guy. I was wondering if I should ask him to the luau or if I should wait for someone to ask me."

"Ah, guy stuff." Alissa nodded. "That'll stress anyone out."

"Ugh, I know." Hannah's shoulders relaxed. "I feel like the guy I want to go with won't ask me even though I want him to. Do you have any advice? Should I go ahead and ask him, or should I drop more hints? Or should I wait for more hints from him?"

Alissa drummed her fingers on the desk underneath her. She was older than Hannah, but in this instance, she didn't feel much wiser. She and Dane communicated well, but she still found him mysterious at times. Like with whatever was going on after hours. She trusted him, but what if she was missing something? They spent so much time together that she found that impossible, but she never knew.

"Honestly, I don't know. I haven't been able to figure men out." She rubbed the back of her neck. "I don't want to lump them all together, but they confuse me too."

Hannah chuckled. "Oh, no. I thought you'd have some secret insights since you have a boyfriend."

"Unfortunately, no. I understand him, but not all of him," Alissa said. "And the men I've dated in the past were hard to figure out too."

"In what way?"

"The guys I dated in the past?" Alissa asked. Hannah nodded eagerly, as if she were waiting for Alissa to bestow some secret knowledge on her. "They were just... not upfront. And even when I asked how they were feeling, they couldn't put what they were feeling to words sometimes. Maybe it was how I was asking, or maybe it was just an age thing. I'm not sure."

Hannah's shoulders slumped for a second until she thought things through.

"I wish there were some key or something to sorting them out." Hannah's eyes danced with amusement. "An eyebrow quirk plus a smile equals interest. A shrug and no eye contact equals no interest."

"Ugh, I wish," Alissa said. "That would make life a whole lot easier, wouldn't it?"

Both women laughed.

CHAPTER TEN

"Can we get a BLT on the fly?" Hannah called back into the kitchen as she passed, her arms weighed down by remnants of a table of five's meals. "There was a seagull incident."

"Again?" Willis said with a sigh. Despite all the signs to not feed the seagulls, someone always threw out a chip or a fry and got swarmed. It had already happened once earlier that morning when some seagulls flew off with someone's whole breakfast sandwich, only to drop it right into the ocean.

"Yep, again." Hannah put the dishes into the sink and washed her hands, looking over her shoulder at the lengthening line. "And we have more customers coming in."

She hustled back to the front counter. The

lunch rush was particularly crazy today, the result of perfect weather and the upcoming weekend. Hannah usually got the chance to breathe, but today it had been order after order, and minor disaster after minor disaster. There were the seagulls, of course, but there were also spills, customers sending orders back for the smallest mistakes, and a chaotic group of tourists who filled the restaurant and changed their minds every five minutes.

Hannah checked the clock. It was only eleven thirty? It felt like she'd gone through an entire day already. She put a smile on her face and greeted the next customer even though she was begging for the rest of the lunch rush to go smoothly. The day couldn't have gotten worse.

Until it did.

Hannah poked the register's touch screen once... then again. Nothing happened, so she stabbed it with her finger until it worked. The customer waiting for her to finish the transaction looked at her and Hannah gave them a nervous smile.

"The system's a little lazy today," she said. She input the customer's chip card and finished the transaction.

Whenever the system got slow, she had to turn it

off and turn it back on again. The process took a few moments, but usually it worked.

"Hi, sorry, just a moment," Hannah said to the next person who stepped up. Luckily they were a regular customer. "We need to restart our system, but I can get your order started. What would you like?"

"Just a crab roll and chips, please."

Hannah scribbled it down and went to the window to hand it to Willis. He picked up the ticket and raised his eyebrow.

"System's restarting," Hannah said. "So we're going old school."

"That computer system." Willis took the ticket and shook his head. "Sometimes technology is more trouble than it's worth. And yes, I know I sound old because I am."

Hannah snorted and went back out to check on the system. It was taking its sweet time rebooting and the line was growing.

"I'll take the next person in line," Hannah said. A tourist came up to the counter. "What can I get you?"

"I'll take a BLT, no tomato, and fries," the man said.

Hannah held in a snort. Her dad was going to get

a kick out of this. Was this a new trend? "Gotcha. Our system is rebooting so I'll ring you up officially once it's back up again."

She scribbled down the order and passed it along to Willis, who looked at the ticket and sighed heavily. Hannah grinned despite the growing line and went back to the computer system. Finally, it was all the way back up again.

She rang up the regular customer with the crab roll and chips, which the system handled with ease. But then, it froze up when she tried to plug in the fact that the customer didn't want tomato. She poked it once. Then again. That got it moving, but when she put in the chip, it skipped back to the beginning of the transaction like nothing had happened.

"Let me try the chip again," Hannah said to the visibly annoyed customer in front of her. "Super sorry about this. Our system is glitchy for some reason."

She inserted the customer's card and prayed it would go through. But instead, she got an error message and the register let out a sad *boop*. Great.

"Do you happen to have cash?" Hannah asked, even though she knew the answer. Most people didn't these days. The customer confirmed it when she shook her head. "I'm so sorry for the inconvenience. Our system is down and we can't take cards at the moment. Since your order is already in the works, it's on the house. "

The customers lined up all sighed and grumbled, and Hannah apologized again.

"What's going on?" Willis called out from the window.

"The computer system is messed up even after I restarted it. There's some error message I've never seen before." Hannah pushed her bangs out of her face and grabbed her phone. "I guess I have to call customer service."

Willis grumbled and came out from the kitchen. "No, they'll leave you on hold for an hour. Can you run down to Sandy's and ask if Luke can come take a look? Sandy said that he straightened out their system. I'll handle everyone here."

"Okay, sure."

"Is anyone paying with cash?" Willis called out to the customers who were lingering.

Thankfully, one or two parties were. Hannah didn't look back to see if they were the only ones. She jogged down to Sandy's, the summer humidity making her sweat right away. Sandy's was busy too, with customers milling around in the aisles. But luckily, Luke was there behind the front counter, working on the computer next to Daniel. Luke waved when he saw her.

"Hey, can I ask you a favor?" Hannah stopped in front of the counter, resting her hands on it and trying to catch her breath. "If you aren't in the middle of something?"

"What's up?"

"The register system at The Crab just went down. Can you help us look at it? It's the middle of lunch rush and we can't take any cards."

Luke looked to Daniel, who nodded as if to say, *go ahead*.

"Yeah, of course," Luke said.

"You're a lifesaver, thank you!"

Hannah and Luke rushed back to The Crab, which now had a sign on the door that said, *Cash Only—System is Down* written in her father's handwriting. Still, the place was packed with customers who had managed to get their orders in before the system went down or customers who paid with cash.

"Dad, we're back," Hannah said to Willis, who was in the back again. "I'll hold down the fort in the front."

"Thanks. A lot of people paid in cash and I'm

getting their orders up as soon as I can," Willis called back.

Luke got to work on the computer while Hannah and Willis tended to the customers. Food came out at a rapid clip once Willis was able to devote all of his time to cooking and Hannah was able to deal with the guests. A few people still came in despite the "cash only" sign on the door and they handled them too. Still, the system being down put them way behind preparing for the dinner rush.

From time to time, Hannah glanced over at Luke, who was deep in concentration at the register, only moving to push his glasses up on his nose. The little furrow in his brow made him look more serious than she ever saw him.

"Yes!" Luke said, grinning and standing up straight. "Fixed it."

"You did?" Hannah whipped around the counter to see. Sure enough, everything looked normal again. "How?"

"I had to uninstall, reinstall, and update something, to not get super technical about it," he said. "If you keep the software updated, which I've automated, you won't run into the issue."

"You're the best, seriously. Thank you so, so

much, Luke. You saved us. Now we just have to catch up on everything."

"It's no problem at all." Luke smiled. "Do you need any more help?"

"Not unless you want to bus tables." Hannah laughed, even though looking out on the utter chaos of the restaurant made her sweat.

"I can do that." He shrugged. "Just tell me where to put stuff."

"Seriously?" Hannah brightened, even through her disbelief.

"Yeah. I'm all yours."

Hannah waited a beat to see if he was kidding, but he wasn't.

"I really, really owe you. Let me get you an apron." Hannah reached under the counter and grabbed one for him. "Let me show you where to put stuff and our system for cleaning."

She guided him over to a table close by and they gathered the dishes, taking them to the dishwashing station. Then, she armed him with a spray bottle of cleaning solution and a rag and showed him the efficient method she used to get it all done. He picked up on it quickly, clearing and cleaning tables. Now that the system was back up and she had taken down the sign on the door, more customers streamed inside.

"You're good on the bussing?" Hannah asked, running her damp hands down her apron.

"Yep, all good." Luke lifted a bin filled with dishes, pushing his glasses up his nose with his arm.

"Thanks!"

Hannah manned the register again, taking orders before going back out to help Luke. He had cleared a bunch of tables in record time.

"Wow, you're fast," Hannah said, finally standing still and taking it all in. "You swoop in, saving the day with the computer and bus the tables like it's nothing? Are you a superhero?"

"I wish." Luke grinned, his smile brightening his whole face. "I'm just your regular neighborhood tech guy."

"What, you aren't hiding a secret identity behind your glasses?" Hannah nudged him with her elbow.

"Nope." He adjusted his thick, dark frames. "And you'd totally know if I took them off because I can hardly see a thing without them."

"Maybe that's what we need to do: put it on hard mode." Hannah smiled at the customers who came in, walking backward toward the register. "No glasses. A restaurant filled with tables to be bussed."

"Only if you try it blindfolded." Luke followed her, stopping on the customer side of the counter. "It'll basically be an even competition."

They both laughed. Luke went outside to check if any of those customers left while Hannah took more orders. Her eyes drifted to Luke when he came back inside, his arms loaded down with empty dishes. His eyes were really nice underneath his thick lenses, bright green and intelligent, framed by long lashes.

And when she thought about the Superman comparison, it worked in a weird way despite him having light brown hair. He had the nerdy exterior of Clark Kent, but he also had a strong jaw that was evident even under his trim beard like Superman. How had she missed how good-looking he was when they first met? Now she couldn't not notice at every angle.

Finally, the lunch rush slowed to a trickle, then a stop. Hannah flopped down into the closest seat and stretched her legs out. She was definitely going to treat herself to a hot bath tonight.

"Is that it? I think that's it," Hannah said, holding up her hand to Luke, who gave her a high-five. "We did it."

"We did."

Luke sat down on the seat next to Hannah's, stretching out as well, his long legs extending past hers. Willis came out of the kitchen, cleaning his hands on a rag.

"Thanks for all your help today," Willis said. "Can I make you something on the house as a thank you?"

"Sure, that would be great. I'd love a fish sandwich and chips," Luke said.

"Coming right up."

Before he left, he shot Hannah a knowing look, his eyes flicking to Luke for a moment. Hannah glared back at him. Her dad had given her that look before back in high school any time a boy even vaguely looked in her direction, but now she was an adult. She didn't want him getting any ideas about intervening. She was more than capable of handling a situation on her own.

Willis finally disappeared into the kitchen, leaving Hannah and Luke alone in the restaurant aside from a couple eating on the far side of the room. They sat in comfortable silence for a while before Hannah noticed the full tip jar and got up.

"Here, let me split these tips up before I forget," Hannah said, reaching into the jar.

"You don't have to do that, Hannah." Luke stood

and crossed toward her in a few long steps. "Seriously. The sandwich is more than enough."

"Come on. Just take it." Hannah started counting out bills and extended them to Luke. He hesitated, then took them, only to put them back into the jar.

"It's fine. It was nice to have an excuse to spend some time with you even though we were running around like crazy," he said, his voice gentle.

Hannah's face heated, then heated more as she took in how he was looking at her. His eyes were soft, like she was the only person he wanted to look at for the rest of the day. It was overwhelming and confusing.

"What is it?" Hannah whispered, her face unbearably warm.

"Nothing. You just look really pretty."

Hannah shook her head, resisting the urge to finger-comb her hair forward to hide her face a little. He had to be flattering her. She was a total mess, red-cheeked, her hair messily falling out of its ponytail, and her shirt smelling of fried food. But the longer he looked at her, the more she realized he was sincere.

He looked at her like she was magical and not just someone who had grown up in Blueberry Bay without having moved anywhere else. Like she wasn't exhausted after a rough day on her feet, fielding problem after problem and scaring away seagulls. She had always felt so ordinary, like she could have blended into any neutral background without anyone looking twice. Never the girl who was the center of anything for anyone.

But Luke didn't see her that way, and it meant more to her than she ever thought it would.

They stood close together, close enough for Hannah to see the faint freckles across his nose even as she looked up at him. His eyes flicked to her lips, then back up to her eyes again. Hannah hadn't kissed a lot of guys, but she knew Luke wanted to kiss her. For a moment, she nearly gave in—the way he made her feel with just a look nearly made her forget the reality of the situation.

She stepped away, unable to look Luke in the eye or figure out what to do with her hands. She wanted to kiss Luke more than she ever thought she would have. But then, Michael still had her attention and she had no idea how he felt about her. Would kissing Luke get around town like all the news did? What if Michael assumed she was taken? But also, she clicked with Luke a lot today... when had she felt like that with a guy? Rarely, if ever.

"Oh, um..." Luke took a step back, his face beet red.

"Uh, yeah." Hannah took another step back too, then turned toward the kitchen. "Thanks again for your help. Let me just... I'm going to go check on your sandwich."

She rushed out, hoping Luke left before she had to face him again.

CHAPTER ELEVEN

Caitlin had come into the kitchen to make herself a cup of tea, but the mug and tea bag sat in front of her, untouched, as she stared out the window. The memory of seeing James and April in the restaurant's office, laughing and standing so close together replayed in her mind over and over any time her brain had a spare moment. Driving, showering, and cleaning up had all become moments to analyze every single part of that moment again.

The way James had smiled, which she hadn't seen him do in a long time. The closeness. The way the office door was open, but was it open enough? She wasn't sure. She had no idea what to do about it, either.

She hadn't mentioned it to James, not because

she was afraid of his reaction, but more that she was afraid of the truth. Of whether she witnessed the final nail in the coffin of her marriage without realizing it.

She finally started the kettle and started washing a few dishes. Along with her replays of the moment came her self-doubt. Had she read into it a little bit too much? Seen something that wasn't there because of her own insecurities? There was always a chance that it was a perfectly harmless interaction.

She poured hot water over her tea bag, her throat tight. Was it really harmless, though? Just because they possibly weren't having an affair? She hadn't seen James look that animated in ages, much less at her. When was the last time he'd looked at her or playfully flirted with her? How was it okay for him to look so relaxed and happy around some other woman when every time they were in the same room felt like being near a stranger? They hardly even spoke.

Her cup of tea was rapidly cooling, so she took it to the living room and pulled out her phone. She called Alissa, hoping she wasn't busy.

"Hey, Caitlin," Alissa said. "What's up?"

"I just..." Caitlin bit the inside of her cheek and tried to think of how to talk about this. "I saw something strange with James. He was talking to one of our suppliers in the office and they were standing close together, talking in a vaguely flirty way. But it could just be nothing. Maybe he was just in a good mood or something..."

Caitlin trailed off, hoping she had made sense. All of the words just came out in a jumble, as if they had a mind of their own when they came out of her mouth. Even though she wasn't sure if she was making any sense, a light weight came off her shoulders after holding all of that in. She hadn't even written about what she had seen in a diary—it had all been clogging up her thoughts.

"I'm sorry, Caitlin. That must have been hard to see," Alissa said softly.

"But you don't think I'm blowing this out of proportion?"

"No, I don't think so. He should be looking at you that way and giving you *some* attention. Even if this woman is a colleague, it sounded like their conversation wasn't all business. Plus, you guys are supposed to be working things out. He should be going out of his way to make you feel like he's still fighting for your family."

Caitlin let her head fall back against the couch. Alissa was right. Besides going to marriage counseling, James hadn't shown that he was taking what they learned to heart. It had just been business as usual, stilted conversations about the most basic things like who was picking up Pearl and who was going to make dinner. No extra time spent together. No signs that she was his wife and not just a woman he lived and worked with.

"Thanks, Alissa," Caitlin said. "That's true. I feel so much better now that I've gotten this off of my chest. I think I'll bring it up with James soon. I can't keep going on like nothing is happening so the only way to resolve it is to face it head on."

"Good. I'll be here for you no matter what."

The weight lifted off her shoulders even more. With Alissa's support, she could get through this.

"Anyway, how are things in Blueberry Bay?" Caitlin asked. "How are things for the luau?"

"Good! Still preparing for the big event. It's all coming together so well." Alissa's energy seemed to drop. "I'm going to be writing something after, which I'm preparing for. Dane still hasn't asked me yet, but it's no big deal. I'm sure he will soon."

"I'm sure he will too."

They caught up about how Pearl was doing in her day camps and what other things were going on in their lives before hanging up.

Caitlin put her phone on the coffee table in front

of her. Even though Alissa had glossed over Dane not asking her to the luau yet, she could tell that it was bothering her. She hoped that they could move past this little rough patch. Dane was a great guy, especially for Alissa. He truly cared about her and wanted her to be happy. She hoped they'd work out. She wanted to believe it was possible.

* * *

Alissa sipped her latte and stretched her other hand out. She had been typing up a storm this morning, working on a long-form article on the luau for the magazine, and her fingers were cramping up. Since she'd already done all the research for the piece, she was flying through the actual writing of it. And that was good too, since she had a whole inbox of emails to attend to also.

Even though it was Saturday, *The Outlet*'s office was busy. Both Josie and Dane were hard at work at their own desks. The paper and the magazine were thriving because of their teamwork, and she was so proud of all the work they'd done.

Alissa rolled her chair a little to the left so she could see Dane through her office window. He was focused on his screen, a slight furrow between his brows. Despite his frown, he was still ridiculously handsome. He had let his rich auburn hair grow out a little, falling slightly onto his forehead but not to the point where it hid his vibrant green eyes. His beard was always so soft under her fingers and she loved tracing the strong angle of his jaw underneath it. She never tired of looking at him, ever, and some days she wondered how she'd lucked out so much.

She turned back to her work with a soft sigh. Dane had always been complimentary of her work, but he was even more so these days. But was he overcompensating for his waning interest in her?

She bit her bottom lip, then cupped her hands around her latte cup for its last remnants of warmth to comfort herself. He still hadn't asked her to the luau even though she'd been dropping hints more and more frequently. Was he not asking her because he didn't think she cared? She hoped that wasn't the case.

After talking with Caitlin, her own anxieties took on a new turn. Had Alissa been brushing things off that were actually significant? What if Josie had feelings for Dane and she was showing it in subtle ways. Or what if Dane had some feelings for Josie that he'd been hiding this whole time, and now Josie was giving off signs that she felt the same way?

Alissa sighed and looked up at the decorations she'd put up. Even though the anxieties behind why Dane hadn't asked her to the luau lingered in the back of her mind, she was still excited for the event.

The front door of the office opened and Alissa leaned over further to see who it was. It was Michael, holding a large iced coffee. He smiled at Josie and brought it over to her. Alissa's eyes widened. Was he making a move on Josie?

Josie thanked him and he turned toward Alissa's office. Alissa straightened up, pretending that she hadn't been watching their interaction with intense interest. Luckily, Michael didn't seem to notice she had been staring.

"Hey, Alissa," Michael said, pulling his phone from his pocket and holding it up. "I just wanted to give you the dates for the upcoming surfing competitions."

"Oh, perfect! Thanks for reminding me. Let me open a document. Just a second." She opened a note on her computer. "Okay, I'm ready."

Michael read off the dates and Alissa took them down. She was excited to attend them. The very first one she had been to was a lot of fun, even in the cold weather. It was a lot like the luau in that people from all over the region came to watch people surf and enjoy all of the small businesses the town had to offer. Michael had won, too, though he had been favored to win by almost everyone.

Alissa had written a few pieces about the event, piquing her interest in the sport. She still hadn't tried it, though.

"Thanks!" Alissa said, saving the dates in a folder on her desktop.

"No problem. I've got to get back to the shop. See you around." Michael nodded to Alissa, then waved to Josie on his way out.

Alissa waited for a few moments before bursting out of her office and into the main entryway where Josie's desk sat. Josie's eyes widened as she sipped her coffee.

"So, when did this thing with Michael start?" Alissa asked with a grin.

"A thing?"

"He brought you coffee. That seems like a big sign that he's interested."

"This?" Josie looked at her coffee and laughed. "It's nothing like that. I ordered some coffee and he offered to bring it over since he had to come give you the dates for the surfing competitions anyway."

"Oh." Alissa's shoulders sagged a little. "Well,

Michael is single and good-looking. Have you ever thought about going out with him?"

She thought about the two of them together, Josie's white blonde hair and delicate features combined with Michael's outdoorsy, laid back energy and dark hair seemed like a perfect match. They would have been a picture perfect couple.

"No, I haven't." Josie sipped her coffee. "Not really. He's not the type of guy I think I'd settle down with. Not that he's a bad guy or anything and from an objective standpoint, I find him handsome. I love living here but I'm a city girl at heart. I don't see myself settling down with a professional surfer, you know?"

"Yeah," Alissa said despite the pit forming in her stomach.

Dane was much more of her type—professional and worldly. Was that what Josie was implying? Their secret meetings came rushing back to Alissa's mind, making the pit in her stomach grow.

"I've got to get back to work," Alissa said, disappearing into her office again.

* * *

"You almost ready, Han?" Willis asked, knocking gently on the bathroom door. "We've got to get going. The breakfast special today is going to take a while to put together."

"Yeah, just a second." Hannah touched up her mascara. She never wore more than that, plus some concealer to work. Anything else would have been sweated off in the first hour of her shift.

She took a step back and looked at herself in the mirror, tilting her head to the side. Fine. She looked just fine. Same dark hair, same fair skin, same brown eyes.

If she were more unique-looking, would Michael take notice? He had been on her mind a lot lately at inopportune times—when she was taking the trash out, talking to customers, or helping her dad prep in the kitchen. She could have done all of those things in her sleep at this point. Her life was that routine.

She came out of the bathroom and grabbed her to-go cup of coffee from the kitchen. Then, she and Willis hopped in his truck to go to The Crab. The familiar route drifted by in the early morning light. Even before she started working at the restaurant, she'd go with her dad in the mornings before she went to school. She knew every part of her town inside and out.

Would she ever know another place as well as she knew this one? It made up so much of who she was—how she viewed the world and moved through it She'd never understand what it was like to live in a place where she didn't know everyone or had to rush everywhere. It sounded hectic, but maybe it was exciting. She had no idea. She hardly knew how people from outside of Blueberry Bay felt about the more mundane things—walking on sidewalks, saying hello to strangers, going out in the evening.

They weren't a big deal at the end of the day, but they were the things that you had to live with every day once the newness of a relationship wore off.

"Do you think it's better to be with someone from the same place as you?" Hannah asked, not taking her eyes off the view from her window. "Or does it not matter?"

"Why do you ask?"

Hannah shrugged. "Just thinking about it. Like how Alissa and Dane both live in Blueberry Bay, but they came from cities. So they understand where the other person came from, which makes them a good match."

Luke popped into her head. He was nice, but he wasn't from around here either. She didn't see herself leaving Blueberry Bay, so they weren't a great match either. But Michael had lived here so long that he was basically as local as she was. Wouldn't that make them a perfect fit? He'd understand her preferring a long walk on the beach instead of going out to a fancy restaurant, or the way she wandered from place to place, taking time to talk to people she knew.

"I think having the same thing in mind for the future is what keeps people together." He tapped his thumb on the steering wheel as they came to a stop at a sign. A hint of sadness came into his eyes. "Your mother came from a completely different world and wasn't content with how life was here. We loved each other, but it wasn't enough in the end. We just saw life differently."

Hannah bit her bottom lip, sadness creeping into her consciousness as well. Her mother leaving had been hard on both of them, and even as a younger person, she recognized how unhappy her mom had become. She always talked about going back to Dallas, where she was from, and most of her parents' arguments were over those little things she had been thinking about before. But when they weren't disagreeing, they seemed to love each other. Love really wasn't going to fix their problems.

She didn't want that future for herself. But being

with Michael was different—they were both suited to the slow pace of small town life. He took it easy, embodying the image of a surfer in almost every way. Even if she felt like life in Blueberry Bay was getting stale, she still liked to take it easy too and probably always would.

But was that enough to push them together? She was still getting mixed signals from him. Maybe all she needed to do was be around him more to see if she could get more clarity about how he felt about her.

CHAPTER TWELVE

Dane paced through his living room, a frown crossing his face. Something felt off with Alissa and he hadn't been able to get to the bottom of it. It was almost like she was avoiding him, and he felt her absence all day. Most Sundays they took a morning walk and sometimes went to the farmers market if it was open. And if they didn't do that, they cooked brunch together at his place since it was a little bigger then curled up together on the couch with their latest reads.

Alissa had gone home a little bit earlier than he had yesterday, claiming she was tired. And she looked tired, so he hadn't called to ask her if they were going to do anything today. So today, he'd spent most of the day alone, puttering around the kitchen and burning toast because he got caught up in what he was reading.

He'd organized his office and gotten some grocery shopping done too. On one hand, he was glad he'd gotten all of that done, but on the other, he wished Alissa were with him as he checked things off his to-do list. Just her presence made the most mundane tasks better.

He pulled his phone out of his pocket and dialed her number. The phone rang for several moments, almost to the point where he was afraid she wasn't going to pick up, but she did at the last minute.

"Hey," Dane said.

"Hi."

"What are you up to?" Dane asked, sitting on the back of his couch.

"Oh, nothing. Just sitting around," Alissa replied, her voice a little flat.

Dane paused, waiting for her to elaborate, but she didn't. Weird. Alissa was almost always doing something, whether it was investigating something in her neighborhood, writing, reading, or trying to make her struggling herb garden work. She could hardly sit still some days.

"Do you want to grab brunch? We haven't been

to Rossi's in a while." He ran his hand through his hair.

"Sure, yeah."

"Great. I'll pick you up in about an hour?"

"Okay. See you then."

He hung up, excited to see her but still uneasy. Was she not feeling well? She still showed up to work yesterday and worked as hard as she usually did.

He took a shower and got dressed, choosing dark jeans and a button-down shirt. Even though Rossi's was one of the nicest restaurants in town, people never dressed up beyond nice jeans. He'd quickly learned that his usual "dressed up" was far too formal for Blueberry Bay.

He drove to Alissa's and texted her when he pulled up. He got out of the car and waited by the passenger door for her, a small knot in his stomach for reasons he couldn't pinpoint. It wasn't the flutter of anticipation he usually felt. Soon, Alissa came out and his breath hitched. No matter how many times he saw her, he was struck by how beautiful she was.

Today she was wearing a navy blue dress he hadn't seen her wear before, her curls forming a halo around her head.

"Hey, you look beautiful," Dane said, giving her a soft kiss.

"Thanks." The corners of Alissa's mouth went up for a moment, but even that small smile didn't reach her eyes. Her smiles always reached her eyes, brightening her entire face.

Dane opened the car door for her and she slid inside. When he got back behind the wheel, he glanced at her and started the car up again. She didn't seem particularly tired or sick. Usually when she got into the car with him, she was bursting to tell him something about her day or something about what was going on in town. Now she was staring blankly out the window.

"Did you have a rough week?" Dane asked, pulling away.

"Mm?" Alissa looked back at him, then out the window again. "No, it was fine. Everything is fine."

Dane raised an eyebrow, but didn't respond. Something clearly wasn't, but he wasn't going to press her in the car. The ride to Rossi's was short and Dane found parking about a block away. Alissa took his hand on the walk over, but much more reluctantly than usual.

Rossi's was busy, but they were seated immediately at a table by the window. The sun was starting to set, illuminating Alissa in golden light. It only served to show what a bad mood she was in.

"What do you think you're going to get?" Dane asked, looking at the menu. "I liked the gnocchi last time but the special sounds good."

"I'm not sure." Alissa frowned at the menu. "The special, I guess."

They sat in awkward silence until the waiter came and took their orders. Dane ordered the wine, as he usually did. Alissa always preferred that he did, but today she even seemed annoyed by that.

"How was your day today?" Dane asked. "Did you do anything fun?"

"It was fine. And I just did some things around my place." Alissa looked past him, then back at the table.

Dane took a deep breath through his nose and let it out.

"What kind of things?" Dane scanned her face.

"Laundry. Did it, folded it. Read a little bit. Wrote a little bit." Alissa dragged her finger through the condensation puddle left behind by her glass of water.

"You wrote some of your new novel?" He sipped his water to dampen his dry mouth. Things had never felt this uncomfortable with Alissa, not even when they first met. "That's great. Did you get over that bit of writer's block you had in the third chapter?"

"Sort of. I just skipped it and started the next chapter."

A long uncomfortable silence stretched out between them. Alissa loved writing novels and usually she couldn't stop talking about it. Then again, her mood often dipped when she hit a creative block. Maybe it was that. He understood. Being stuck on a creative problem was always so difficult. You couldn't force it.

Sometimes Alissa talked about the problem she was having and bounced ideas off of him, but today she stayed quiet. A simmer of frustration started to build in his gut, but he set it aside.

"I really love your features on the luau," he said. Work was usually a safe topic no matter what, but today, Alissa's eyes narrowed in uncharacteristic anger.

"Some couples have time to enjoy actually going to events like that. Together." Alissa's hand formed a fist on the table, like she was holding on in fear of losing control. "But it feels like you've been so busy that you don't have time for the luau or me."

Dane sat back in his seat, blinking several times.

He had never seen Alissa this upset before, and it seemed like it had come out of nowhere.

"Alissa, what brought this on?" Dane kept his voice soft, resisting the urge to take her hand across the table. Touching her was probably the last thing she wanted from him.

Alissa sighed, her eyes watery. "You've just been so... you've been staying late at the office and then there are these lunches with Josie that don't make any sense. And I keep trying to get you into the luau and drop hints about you asking me, but you haven't yet. It's like I'm just a walking, talking set of articles to you and not your girlfriend."

Alissa's voice cracked on her final words and she pushed her glasses up on her nose. Dane opened his mouth, then closed it when he realized he didn't know what to say. He didn't *feel* like he was spending less time with Alissa. He just felt like he was trying to get ready for the luau by learning to hula. But he didn't want to ruin the surprise.

"Alissa, it's..." Dane still found himself at a complete loss for words. "I don't..."

"You're right. You didn't." Alissa stood up and grabbed her purse, storming out.

Dane felt as if someone had dumped ice water down the back of his shirt. He raked his hand down his face and groaned. How had he not seen how ignored Alissa felt? He still had no idea what to say to make it right, as much as he wanted to.

* * *

Hannah tightened her ponytail as she walked to Tidal Wave Coffee. She almost never went there on a Sunday in the middle of the day, but she was going with a purpose—trying to get a better feel of how Michael felt for her. And getting some coffee and croissants for her and her friend Jessie from high school while she was at it.

She knew he was frequently there on the weekend to manage things and prepare for the upcoming week. Hopefully he wasn't changing his routine.

The shop wasn't too busy. There were a few people grabbing pastries and coffees for light Sunday brunches, but no one was in line. Luckily, Michael was there with one of his baristas behind the espresso machine. His eyes were bright with excitement, which gave him a boyish charm that Hannah rarely saw on his face.

She hesitated for a moment, but stepped inside.

"Hey, just the person I wanted to see!" Michael said.

Hannah looked over her shoulder to see if he was talking to someone behind her, but he was talking to her. Her face heated up immediately and she smiled a little.

"Really?" Hannah asked.

"Yeah. Just a second." Michael did something with the machine and came toward the bar. "You mentioned you like oat milk, right? We've been messing around with some drinks for the luau and I was wondering if I could get your opinion."

"Oh, sure." Hannah wasn't sure whether this was a good sign or not, but he'd specifically called her out for this. "What is it?"

Michael slid a small cup across the bar.

"It's a toasted coconut latte. I know it seems like we should use all coconut milk, but it's slightly too rich." Michael rested his forearms on the high bar. "The oat milk is creamy but not too creamy."

Hannah sniffed it—it smelled like drinking a coffee on the beach—and took a sip. It was delicious and tasted exactly as it smelled. She nodded and gave a thumbs up.

"It's super good!" Hannah said. "I'd definitely drink this. It's rich but not so rich that I'd feel like taking a nap or sitting down after. I bet it would be good over ice too."

"That's exactly what I wanted to hear." Michael smiled. "Hold on just a second—let's make one over ice and see if it's just as good."

Michael went back behind the espresso machine to work with his barista. She looked down at the floor, trying to suppress the huge grin spreading across her face. Even though he was working with his barista, this felt like something that was special between the two of them. How many other people had he asked to taste this latte? Not many, if she had to guess. And he valued her opinion.

"Okay, toasted coconut latte over ice," Michael said, sliding another small cup to Hannah.

She sipped it, her face hot as Michael watched her every move. It was delicious too.

"Just as good. Maybe even better." Hannah gave him another thumbs up, momentarily feeling dorky until Michael returned it.

"Perfect. Want an iced one on the house for being a great taste tester?" Michael asked.

"Oh, you don't have to do that."

"No, I insist. Unless you were dead set on something else to drink." Michael paused with his hand on the stack of clear cups next to the bar.

"I was just going to get something for me and a friend," Hannah said.

"So two iced toasted coconut lattes on the house." Michael said with a broad smile that made Hannah's heart flip over in her chest. "It's the least I can do."

"Okay, sure. Thank you." Hannah bit her bottom lip, feeling fidgety.

Hannah watched him walk the barista through making the lattes, her thoughts racing so fast that she couldn't decipher any of them. She had so much to ask Jessie about when they hung out.

"Here you go. Anything else?" Michael asked, tucking the drinks into a caddy for her.

"Two chocolate croissants would be great." Hannah pulled out her wallet. "And I insist on paying for those."

Michael went over and rang her up while the barista grabbed the croissants for her.

"Thanks again for being my taste tester," Michael said, still smiling.

"Yeah, any time." Hannah smiled back and left, feeling a new lightness in her step.

She walked all the way down to the boardwalk near a spot where she and Jessie had met up frequently since high school. Even though the spot wasn't near anything specific, Hannah could have found it in her sleep. Every part of the boardwalk was familiar to her, even the spots where the wood was a little bit worn through.

She spotted Jessie's curly dark hair sitting on their favorite bench and sat down next to her. They had been friends since middle school, staying close through their awkward teenaged years. Jessie had gone to the community college a thirty minute drive away for two years and like most people Hannah had grown up with, had returned to Blueberry Bay to work for a small real estate office.

Out of all her friends, Jessie was the best person to talk to about problems with guys. She had dated around more than Hannah had—not that Hannah had dated much at all—and now had a boyfriend, a guy she had met through a friend from college. He was a nice guy, the kind of boyfriend that most people probably wanted: attentive and kind.

"Hey!" Jessie said, only slightly startled at Hannah's sudden appearance. She took a latte. "Thanks for breakfast."

"Yeah, no problem." Hannah handed Jessie a croissant too and rested her coffee on the wooden ledge acting as a barrier between the edge of the boardwalk and the sand below. "It's a toasted coconut latte."

Jessie stabbed her straw into the cup and took a sip, eyes widening as she swallowed.

"That's amazing," Jessie said, taking a longer sip. "Is this new?"

"Yeah. I was the official taste tester and Michael gave them to me for free." Hannah laced her words with meaning.

"*Oh.*" Jessie had also worked for Tidal Wave Coffee while she was taking classes at the community college, so she was very familiar with both Michael and Hannah's crush on him. "Wow. Both of these? Free?"

"Yeah." Hannah sipped hers. "So the other day, I was just getting a coffee like I usually do and he asks if I like oat milk. Then I came in today so I could see Michael and get a better sense of how he feels about me, and he asks me to be his taste tester, like I said. He seemed so enthusiastic and happy to see me. That has to be a good sign, right?"

"Yeah. It's not a *bad* sign." Jessie broke off part of her croissant and popped it into her mouth, chewing thoughtfully.

"Did Michael ever have customers taste test things?"

"Not that I can remember, but I never worked there around the luau. But he was pretty strict about not giving friends freebies, so maybe he does feel something for you."

Hannah's heart pounded and her body heated up so much that the chocolate of her croissant seemed to melt in her mouth even faster. Having Jessie's perspective gave her hope, but then she remembered her other issue.

"There's a little knot in this situation," Hannah said. "Do you know Luke? Sandy and Daniel's nephew?"

"Of course. He's the one who's fixed like, half the gadgets and computers in town already." Jessie snorted, pushing a curl out of her face. "Wasn't he helping out at The Crab?"

Growing up with her friends in a small town was a double-edged sword. On one hand, people knew you through thick and thin, through every awkward phase. They understood Hannah in ways that people she'd become friends with as an adult didn't.

But on the other, having a secret was near impossible. She trusted Jessie, of course, but if Luke was connected to Sandy and Daniel, then Jessie might bring up Luke if someone mentioned Sandy's Grocery. Not in a malicious way of course, but in a way that would get the rumor mill rolling. Sometimes just having a droplet of information created a whole flood.

Hannah sighed, chewing on her straw. Things could be worse, she supposed. They didn't fully kiss. And Luke was a nice guy. But what if Michael heard and thought that Hannah was taken? It didn't matter —she wanted Jessie's input on the situation more than she was worried about news of it getting around.

"He did. He was super helpful and we kind of hit it off. But then we nearly kissed and it was... I don't know."

"What?" Jessie gently smacked Hannah with the back of her hand. "Why didn't you text me right away?"

"We didn't actually kiss, so I didn't think it was that big of a deal." Hannah lifted one shoulder. "But it was awkward since I decided not to at the last minute."

"Did you not want to kiss him?"

"That's the thing. I don't know. It felt right at the time until I got into my head about it." Hannah ran her fingers through the end of her ponytail. "I was thinking about how much I like Michael and I wouldn't want him to think I wasn't interested if people found out."

"Ah." Jessie nodded in understanding.

"So I think I should try to make a move on Michael and ask him to the luau, especially if you think that he's giving out positive signals." Hannah bit her bottom lip. "But the problem is, is it enough?"

"He doesn't have to be in love with you already. He just has to be interested enough to get to know you more," Jessie said. "I think you should go for it. What do you have to lose?"

"Oh, um, a lot?" Hannah huffed a laugh even though the idea of getting shot down made her sweat profusely.

"Or you could get a date to the luau with a great guy." Hannah finished off her croissant. "If you don't take the shot, how do you know if you would have made it or not?"

Jessie was right. Hannah was going to ask Michael to the luau. She'd kick herself if she missed the chance.

CHAPTER THIRTEEN

Hannah's outfit options were limited—she had her red t-shirt with The Crab's logo on it, or her dark blue t-shirt with The Crab's logo on it. But instead of her usual denim shorts, she chose a denim skirt that she could still move around in, and took extra time in doing her makeup and hair.

She wound her dark hair around her curling iron and released it, tugging it and letting it bounce. It had taken her an extra twenty minutes, but she thought she looked much nicer than usual. That gave her the boost of confidence she needed. She was going to Tidal Wave Coffee to ask Michael to the luau before work, just as Jessie had urged her to do.

Willis had left earlier than her to sign for a delivery, so she hopped in her car and drove off to the coffee shop. She put on her most upbeat, motivational music, trying to keep her spirits up despite her rapidly pounding heart. Any progress she made on that front disappeared the moment she walked into the shop and saw Michael there, talking to one of his baristas behind the counter.

He was dressed in a wetsuit, like he was going to go out surfing after making sure his barista was set up for the day.

Hannah swallowed, resisting the urge to play with her hair as she walked up to them.

"Hi, Hannah," Michael said with a smile. "How are you?"

"Not bad." Hannah cleared her throat. "Can I talk to you for a second?"

"Sure, of course." He walked around the counter.

"Can I make you anything while you talk?" the barista asked.

"Sure, an oat milk latte would be great. Thank you." Hannah paid for her drink, then went over to the table where Michael was waiting for her.

He looked way too handsome for her to focus on her goal. His dark, wavy hair was pulled back out of his face, showing off his high cheekbones and stubbled jaw. For a moment she nearly backed out, but she sat down and took a deep breath.

"What's going on?" Michael asked, the easy smile that made Hannah's heart flutter spreading across his face.

The words that she had rehearsed over and over again since she got the courage to ask Michael to the luau disappeared from her head entirely. She cleared her throat again and tried to recover.

"So, I was just... I just wanted to tell you that I like you a lot. And I know that you might not have wanted to ask me out or anything like that since we basically only know each other from around town and from the time you saved me. But I hope we can get to know each other more," Hannah said. It was more or less what she had rehearsed in her head, and it had come out smoother than she thought it would, given how nervous she was.

Michael didn't respond, so Hannah kept going.

"So, would you like to go to the luau?" Hannah asked. "With me, I mean."

Michael took a deep breath, shifting in his seat. "Thank you for telling me. And for asking me. While I think you're very nice, I'm not interested in being anything more than friends."

Hannah froze, wishing an actual tidal wave would wash her away. Mortification didn't cover the level of embarrassment she felt. How had she gotten it so wrong? How was she going to ever look Michael in the eye ever again? She had spent hours and hours of analyzing every single interaction they ever had for clues and apparently, she hadn't seen the forest for the trees.

"Oat milk latte on the bar," the barista called.

"I have to get to work," Hannah sputtered, standing up so quickly that her chair squeaked on the hardwood floor. "My drink is ready. Bye."

She snatched the drink off the bar and hustled out to her car, hoping Michael didn't notice how red her face had gotten.

Luke gently placed a box of the latest shipment of cereal down to be loaded onto a pallet and stocked on the shelves. He didn't mind unloading or shelving, especially since he could usually listen to his music or a podcast as he worked. But today, he couldn't keep his mind from wandering back to Hannah. Everything seemed to remind him of her— certain songs, mundane items, customers who he spotted out of the corner of his eye who looked like her.

He sighed, going for the next box. He'd blown it

with her by nearly kissing her. Every time he thought about it, his neck got hot. Thinking about it now, he wondered what he had been running through his head. But in the moment, it had felt right. He thought she was showing some interest, with her big smiles and the way they laughed together. And he could have sworn she had leaned in, just a little bit.

But apparently not. Or more accurately, her feelings for Michael were stronger. He wanted to kick himself. It all felt so obvious. Now what was he going to do? He loved The Crab's food but he didn't want to make things awkward by going there and ordering a sandwich. What would he have said to her? *Sorry for almost kissing you?*

"Hey, Luke," Sandy said, appearing in the doorway to the back. "How's it going?"

"Not bad." He stood up straight, stretching his back.

"You've gotten so much done." Sandy put her elbow on a stack of boxes that were almost as tall as she was. "It's nice having you around here. And not just for the extra help."

"I like it here too," Luke said.

"Enough to stick around?"

"No. I don't think it's for me in the long run. It's nice to absorb the quiet and the slower pace for a little while, but I think I like a faster pace for my everyday life." He shrugged. "Plus, I don't know if I'd ever find a girl who I could relate to if I stayed here long term. We'd probably want different things."

Sandy raised an eyebrow, a hint of a smile coming onto her lips.

"Oh? What do you mean by that?"

Luke cupped the back of his neck. "Well, you know when I went over to help at The Crab after their system went down. Hannah and I worked together for most of that afternoon and I thought we hit it off. I know I'm starting to feel for her."

He paused, debating whether to tell Sandy that they almost kissed. The thought made his whole body feel even hotter, so he decided against it. He was shoving that embarrassing moment in his mental vault, where it would inevitably pop into his head at inopportune times and make him cringe.

"But basically, I think I read her wrong and she has feelings for someone else." Luke sighed. "I don't know what to do now. What *should* I do? Or should I just leave it and pretend it didn't happen?"

"I think you should be honest with her. Clear the air and make sure she's actually feeling what you think she's feeling. Maybe she doesn't see it the way you're seeing it," Sandy said. "It's pointless to ruin what could be a friendship even if it was an awkward situation. Think about it. You've probably had awkward moments with your friends a bunch of times. Now you don't even think about them all that much."

Luke absently scratched at his beard as he thought Sandy's words through. He did like her. It had been a while since he'd had feelings like this for someone—that flutter in his gut, the warmth that spread through him when she smiled at him. Being just friends with someone who he had those kinds of feelings for wasn't something he'd done before.

But he did enjoy Hannah's company. And letting that slip by seemed like something he'd regret.

"That's true," Luke said. "I'll try to clear the air with her."

CHAPTER FOURTEEN

The temperature in the office seemed to drop by several degrees when Dane came in from a brief break outside. He and Alissa locked eyes, but Alissa looked back at her computer, her back tense. Josie looked between the two of them, her eyes wide.

Dane nodded in greeting and went to his office without a word.

Alissa sighed through her nose and tried to focus again. They hadn't spoken much since she left Rossi's and the more time passed, the more confused she felt. And the more hurt. He had genuinely been confused when she told him how she felt. She hadn't thought he'd respond that way at all. She figured he'd either explain everything that was going on, or at least apologize for how much he'd been ignoring her lately.

She hadn't intended to storm off like that, but she was so overwhelmed that she couldn't sit there and pretend she was okay any longer. She had walked and walked until she found herself back at home. After sending Dane a text telling him that she was okay, she had curled up in bed, questions preventing her from slipping off into sleep.

Her confusion lingered until Dane stepped out to get coffee. Not having him across the hall let her relax. Josie appeared in her doorway, tapping on the door frame.

"Hey." Josie leaned against the frame, concern on her face. "Is everything all right?"

Alissa took off her glasses and cleaned them on the bottom of her shirt before putting them back on.

"Not really. It's just that..." Alissa paused, trying to think of how to frame her questions. Josie knew both of them, so there was no use in pretending this wasn't about her and Dane. "Is it normal for a man to get cold feet about asking his girlfriend to an event? It seems like it's a given that they'd go together, but still, someone has to ask the other person, right?"

Josie nodded, biting her plush bottom lip for a moment. "I'd say so. But I know for a fact that Dane is head over heels for you, so if he's getting cold feet, it's probably temporary. I don't think he's losing feelings for you."

That wasn't the answer she was expecting from Josie either. In fact, her being there was sort of strange now that Alissa thought about it. She figured that she and Dane were having some sort of affair behind her back. Why was Josie so calm and collected about all of this? Wouldn't she have been at least slightly uncomfortable?

"Thanks, Josie," Alissa said.

"No problem."

Josie went back to her desk, leaving Alissa more confused than ever. Josie wasn't the type to lie easily. If she were hiding this big affair right under Alissa's nose, Alissa felt as if she'd know. But then again, what if she was wrong and Josie *was* hiding something?

Still, that didn't feel right to her. She had more questions than she had answers.

* * *

Dane glanced at the clock, breathing a sigh of relief that the day was almost over. It had been a long one filled with awkward interaction after awkward interaction. Conversations that he usually loved going to Alissa's office for were done over email, drawing them out three times as long as usual. He had to plan when to get up to get water because he didn't want to bump into Alissa.

It was exhausting. And Alissa wasn't at all like the woman he had fallen for, at least not at that moment. Her distance hurt even more now that they had to be in the same office. At least Alissa had gone home for the day so her distance wasn't smacking him in the face every fifteen minutes.

"Hey, did you want to have another dance lesson tonight?" Josie asked, resting her hand on the door frame of Dane's office.

"I'm not really in the mood." He ran his hands through his hair. "Alissa and I aren't really getting along at the moment anyway."

Josie glanced over her shoulder and stepped inside of his office, shutting the door behind her.

"I could guess that from how you guys went from chatting all the time to barely wanting to stand in the same room as each other," Josie said. "I spoke with Alissa earlier and she asked about whether you were getting cold feet."

Dane frowned, his eyes narrowing. Cold feet? About their relationship? He didn't think things were that bad. Josie caught on to his confusion and gave him a patient smile.

"I think Alissa has caught on to us spending more time together for your dance lessons," Josie said. "And I think she probably thinks you're losing interest in her since we're spending time together and you're being secretive about what you're doing."

Dane stared blankly at Josie, wondering why he hadn't put all the pieces together. It made so much sense that he was kicking himself for not getting it sooner. How had he not seen how his lessons with Josie had come off? A man and a woman spending time together in secret would raise flags for anyone, really.

"Should I tell her what's going on so she's not upset?" Dane asked.

Josie lifted one shoulder in a shrug. "I mean, it's up to you, but you've come this far. The luau is soon and she'll love the surprise. She'll be so thrilled to see you do it and she'll forgive you on the spot. She still has feelings for you so she won't end things."

Dane considered it. Alissa loved surprises and she loved it when he got outside of his comfort zone. If he held onto his secret for just a little while longer, it could be amazing. But he didn't want her to continue feeling so bad. He never intended to hurt her.

"Okay, let's keep going on the path we were on. But we have to be more subtle about meeting up so we won't hurt Alissa's feelings," Dane said. "And I'll be more intentional about showing her I care in the meantime."

"Sounds like a plan."

CHAPTER FIFTEEN

The walk from Sandy's to The Crab wasn't long, but Luke drew it out as much as he could. He was sweating from both the evening warmth and his nerves at the conversation he was about to have with Hannah. Rehearsing what he was going to say over and over again helped, but also made him overanalyze everything.

All he had to do was apologize for misreading her. That was it.

He finally rounded the corner to The Crab. The sign was off, but he heard the sounds of gentle piano playing coming from inside the open door between the inside of the restaurant and the patio. He came closer and saw Hannah at the piano, playing a beautiful, but melancholy song. It was so complex, chords perfectly in sync and creating a mood that filled the air.

Her expression matched the music, though, to his dismay, her brows furrowed. Still, he sat down at one of the tables outside just to listen.

Hannah was so swept up in the music that she didn't notice Luke at all until she came to a slower part. She jumped a little and stopped, her cheeks pink.

"Don't stop," he said. "I hope you don't mind that I was eavesdropping."

"It's all right." She gestured vaguely to the open door. "I'm sort of outside anyway."

"You're really good." Luke glanced over the piano. It was older, but well-maintained. "How long have you been studying music?"

"Oh, I haven't really studied it. At least officially." Hannah looked down at her hands, her cheeks darkening even more. "I took lessons from someone around here when I was younger, but I outgrew that. Now I just mess around and compose stuff after hours. I watch videos on music theory sometimes if I want to understand how to create a certain sound too."

"You composed that? What you were just playing?" Luke blinked. "That's incredible, Hannah.

You're really talented. I thought that was some popular song I just happened to miss out on."

Her hands went to her cheeks, as if covering them could stop her from blushing. It was incredibly cute and made his heart flip in his chest. Well, until he remembered that he was here to put those feelings aside, which put a damper on the feeling.

"Thank you. Sorry, I'm bad at taking compliments," Hannah said.

"I get it. I'm not sure if anyone is." He smiled. "Have you ever thought about going to school for it?"

Hannah paused, biting her bottom lip and absently scratching her forearm. "I mean, yeah. But that's as far as it's gotten—my thoughts."

"Is it more because you aren't interested, or... ?"

"I'm interested still." Hannah looked past Luke's shoulder. "But it's not like Blueberry Bay is a popular spot for music schools. I'd have to leave and I don't want to leave my dad here with The Crab. I mean, I know he's totally capable of running the place, but..."

Luke watched her gather her thoughts. She raked her fingers through her long ponytail, her gaze getting far away.

"I don't know. It's complicated. I don't want to be like my mom." Hannah frowned, like she wasn't sure how her words sounded to someone else.

"What happened with her?"

"She and my dad split up because she didn't like life here, basically. It really put a strain on their relationship so she just left." Hannah shrugged. The way she talked about it made it sound like she was over it, though Luke imagined it must not have been. "I know I'm not, but if I left, I'd be like her in that way. She left and didn't look back. And as much as my dad tries to keep a brave face on, I know that it still hurts. He loved her very much."

"I bet," Luke said softly.

"Yeah. So it doesn't really feel like I can leave without hurting him and we're really close." Hannah skimmed her fingers over the piano keys without pressing them down. "So I guess my music will just be here as an outlet for my feelings, happy or sad. More like the latter tonight."

Luke hesitated. He'd read into her feelings a little too much before and made assumptions, but this felt like something he could talk to her about. She had opened up to him about some deep feelings.

"What were you playing through tonight?" Luke asked.

"Oh, gosh." Hannah pressed down two keys. "It's mortifying, but I told Michael how I felt about him and asked him to the luau. He told me he only saw me as a friend. I grabbed my coffee and booked it out of there before I passed out from embarrassment right there on the floor. Then Michael would have had to save me twice."

"I'm sorry." He had been turned down before and it never felt good, even if the rejection was gentle. "But you shouldn't feel bad in the long run. It's not like him turning you down is a reflection on who you are as a person. It's his loss that he can't see how wonderful you are."

Luke swallowed, his face getting hot. His words had been way, way too earnest and she saw his meaning right away. Why hadn't he learned his lesson before? His excess enthusiasm was the whole reason he'd gone to The Crab in the first place.

"Sorry." Luke messed with his beard, then put his hands in his lap so he wouldn't fidget. But that only made him feel more awkward. "I should apologize for the other day too. I was way too forward and read your signals wrong."

"It's okay. You don't have to apologize for that." Hannah tucked a loose strand of hair behind her ear. "I was swept up myself, but clearly a little too much. I got too blinded by my puppy crush to see someone who was noticing me."

Her smile was warm, making the same feeling

spread through his belly. He felt like the one who was swept up this time. Hannah's beautiful, petite features glowed in the low light, making it impossible for him to take his eyes off of her.

"I understand that too," he said, clearing his throat.

Hannah got up and sat next to him, only a few inches between them. Luke's skin tingled even though they weren't touching.

"If you ever tried to kiss me again, I'd definitely accept it," Hannah said, leaning closer to him.

Luke grinned. That was all the invitation he needed. He took Hannah's hand in his and kissed her softly on the lips. It was sweet, tasting like mint, and better than he'd ever dreamed. She squeezed his hand in the middle of it. The grip of her small hand in his was the perfect reminder that yes, this was actually happening.

They broke apart, grinning at each other, their fingers still twined together.

CHAPTER SIXTEEN

"PJ time!" Caitlin said to Pearl. "Which ones do you want to wear?"

"The pink ones." Pearl went on her tiptoes and pulled them out of her dresser drawer.

Pearl changed into them and Caitlin straightened the fabric, and luckily, Pearl hopped right into bed, a smile on her face.

"Can you read me a story?" Pearl asked, reaching for one of the books in the basket she kept near her bed.

"Sure, pick one." Caitlin sat on Pearl's bed, already knowing which one she was going to pick.

Pearl picked the book that Caitlin expected—the story of a princess and her pet dragon. Even though Pearl was several grade levels ahead in her reading skills, Pearl still loved the ritual of being read to before falling asleep. Caitlin loved it too.

Caitlin tucked the blankets around Pearl before opening up the book, holding it so Pearl could see the pictures. They had read it before bed so many times that Caitlin was able to recite it by heart. She had her silly voices down, which always made Pearl laugh no matter what.

Since the book was short, they read another one before Pearl's eyelids started to get heavy. Eventually Pearl was asleep, her face relaxed. Caitlin turned off the lamp, put the book back in the basket, and kissed Pearl on the forehead.

Caitlin slipped out of Pearl's room. The sense of happiness and peace she felt being around her daughter disappeared and her stomach tightened. She had to talk to James about what she saw tonight, or she'd lose the nerve.

She went into the living room, where James was watching a cooking reality show and working on some supplier forms on his laptop.

"Hey," Caitlin said, sitting down next to him. In the past she would have been comfortable sitting pressed up against him, but she kept a lot of space between the two of them.

"Hi." James glanced at her for a moment before looking back at the TV, then at his laptop again.

"Can we talk?"

"Can we talk about it later? Maybe in the morning?" James asked, still looking at his laptop. "I have a lot to do."

"It's important." Caitlin swallowed. "It can't wait."

James raised his eyebrows. "Okay, go ahead."

"The other day I saw you talking to April in the restaurant's office," Caitlin said, keeping her voice as steady as possible. "And I couldn't help but notice that you two seemed close. Is there something going on between you two?"

James finally closed the laptop and put it on the coffee table, his expression getting serious. Finally, Caitlin had his full attention.

"I'd never cheat on you, Caitlin," he said. "Our vows mean something to me and I'd never sleep with someone else."

She wanted his words to bring her relief, but they didn't. Something about the way he said it was only making her stomach tighten even more.

"Okay," Caitlin said, her voice weak.

James ran a hand through his hair, his brows furrowed.

"But... I've developed some feelings for her," he added. "We've become close and she understands my drive to expand the business. To put my all into it. I can't deny that connection."

Caitlin felt as if someone had dropped a weight on her stomach. The idea of actually responding to him verbally was impossible. She couldn't even gather the words in her mind.

"But I've never cheated. It's just feelings," James said.

Caitlin was numb. All she could do was nod. With all of the distance that had grown in between them, the idea of divorce had flitted into her head. But now it was a reality—her marriage was over.

The show on TV switched over to a loud, cheerful laundry detergent commercial. Caitlin grabbed the remote and turned it off.

"I know you didn't cheat and I believe you there," Caitlin said after clearing her throat. "But it's clear that you don't want the things that our marriage is giving you. If you can only feel a special connection with someone who isn't me, that's a problem."

James ran his hands through his hair again, his expression sober. "I agree."

The ache in her chest grew and grew until it felt as if it were overflowing.

"I'm hurt that this didn't come up earlier in counseling," she said, her courage growing just enough. "I deserve better than that."

"I know. You do." James turned toward her more. "So what do you propose we do?"

The lump in her throat was overwhelming and a tear slipped out of her eyes.

"We should probably separate while we figure out how to proceed," Caitlin said. "And then we could go forward with a divorce."

James was teared up too, but his didn't fall. "That sounds like the best way. And we can figure out how to break this to Pearl."

Caitlin's heart clenched, thinking of her little girl peacefully asleep, unaware of what was happening. James ran his hand up and down her upper back when he saw her face. It was the kind of comfort she'd craved for months, but now it was too late.

"I don't know how we're going to do that," Caitlin admitted.

"I don't know either." James blew out a breath. "But however we decide to do it, we have to tell her that we still love her very much."

"Definitely."

They sat in silence again, the weight of the fact that their marriage was over taking up all the air in the room.

Hannah sliced through a pineapple, one of many that she'd had to cut in preparation for the luau. It wasn't crunch time yet, but they were finalizing parts of the menu during the lull in the lunch rush. It was all coming together well. They just had to make sure everything was perfect and easy to prep.

"Can I taste that pineapple before we grill it?" Willis asked.

"Is that just an excuse to eat more pineapple?" Hannah snorted. Her father had been nibbling on more pineapple than he had the other elements of their recipes. "We can eat those separately, you know. We got plenty."

Willis grumbled and took a slice of pineapple, popping it into his mouth.

Hannah smiled and ate a little bit herself. Willis took one large round slice and tossed it on the grill. It was going to be a part of their Hawaiian burger. As it cooked, Willis threw a burger patty on the other side of the grill and peered through the window to see if any customers had come up.

"Luke was a lifesaver fixing our software system," Willis said. "We haven't had any problems with it since."

Hearing Luke's name made Hannah's cheeks heat immediately. Her mind had drifted to their kiss all morning, making her feel light and airy every time.

"Yeah, he's very nice," she replied, trying to sound as casual as possible and failing miserably. Willis's craggy eyebrows went up. "What?"

"Are you getting to know each other?" Willis asked.

"I don't know." Hannah lifted a shoulder since she truly wasn't sure. She hoped to see him again soon

The sizzling of the grill was the only sound that stretched between them for a few moments.

"You don't have to hold back on dating on my account," Willis finally said. "I feel bad that you might have felt like you couldn't date because we're so busy with the restaurant. You've hardly dated."

Hannah blinked in surprise. She never thought he blamed himself for that. While they were busy, he always gave her time off to hang out with a friend or just to rest when she asked for it.

"Don't blame yourself." Hannah rested a hand on the prep table and snagged another small slice of pineapple. "I probably haven't dated much just because Blueberry Bay is so small. No one has really caught my interest."

She felt like she knew every single guy her age, and she had gone to high school with every last one of them. And many of them were nice and some had even asked her out on dates, but she had turned them down. She hadn't been drawn to many of them at all. But she had been drawn to Luke, even if she'd been too caught up in her crush on Michael at first to notice it.

Fortunately, things didn't seem to be too awkward between her and Michael, which was good, since they saw each other often around the small town. And she was starting to truly understand that her feelings for him had been nothing but puppy love, unlike the deeper connection she shared with Luke. Now Luke was the center of her thoughts, and every time he came to mind, she couldn't help the smile that broke out across her face.

"I do like Luke a lot," she admitted to her father.

"He's different than any guy I've ever known, and we have the best time together."

"You should get to know him better, then," Willis said. "He's not from around here, so he might be the right one for you."

"I think I will."

The knot that had been in her stomach without her even knowing it loosened a bit as she grinned at her father. Having his blessing meant the world to her.

* * *

Alissa gazed at the vase of flowers that Dane had surprised her with that morning. They were gorgeous, a mix of peonies and some of her other favorites, and made her whole office smell great. She inhaled and blew out a sigh as guilt crept into her consciousness again.

Maybe she had been too harsh on Dane with her doubts. He had been so attentive lately—the flowers, little notes, her favorite overcomplicated caramel latte from Tidal Wave Coffee. Maybe she was overreacting. He clearly still cared about her.

She turned her attention back to her article, which she had stayed late to wrap up. It was one of the final promotional articles on the luau, and in her opinion, it was one of her best. With a few more sentences she was done. She sent it off to Dane, who happened to walk into the office moments later.

"I just sent off my article to you," she said.

"Good." He walked across her office, gently massaging the back of her neck.

"A little to the left... perfect." Alissa sighed as his fingers worked through a knot. "I swear, I don't know why I'm so surprised that my neck hurts everyday when I sit at my desk curled up like a shrimp."

Dane chuckled, leaning down and kissing her on the forehead. "I don't know either, but I'm here to help."

"Thank you." She smiled up at him as he perched on her desk. "Why are you still here? Still working on the latest issue?"

"Yeah. And I just wanted to come in and see you before you left." The warmth and affection in his eyes made Alissa's insides melt. She reached for his hand and he took it, squeezing her softly.

"You did?"

"I did. I just wanted to tell you how much you mean to me." He traced a line down the back of her hand with his thumb. "And how much I appreciate you opening me up to Blueberry Bay."

Alissa held her breath for a moment, waiting for him to finish off the sweet sentiment with an invitation to the luau or at least something about it. But he didn't. As touched as she was at the sentiment, she couldn't help her stomach from sinking a little in disappointment. He might have said he had opened up to the town, but it didn't seem like he was embracing one of its biggest traditions.

CHAPTER SEVENTEEN

Luke had wanted to sleep in more on his day off, but he woke up around eight instead. He'd gotten so used to waking up early from working at the store that his body couldn't let him rest more if he tried. It didn't matter, though. He had plans for the day, plans that made his palms sweat just thinking of them, so he figured diving into the day would be a better idea than sitting back and worrying about it.

He stretched and yawned, getting out of bed and brushing his teeth. Sandy and Daniel's house was quiet, the view of lush green trees out the window above the kitchen sink adding to the calm energy the entire town had. His stomach growled and he opened the fridge to find something to eat. The best thing about working for the store was that he never had to run to get something on his way home—the fridge was always stocked.

He pulled out some eggs, cheese, onion, and bell peppers for a quick omelet. Being nervous always made him more hungry, as paradoxical as it sounded to others. He needed a full stomach to go talk to Hannah at The Crab or he'd feel sick.

After finding the cutting board, Luke started chopping up the peppers, his mind racing. He knew the general idea of what he was going to say. He wanted to talk to her about pursuing her passions. But how? He didn't want to come across as pushy. Even though they'd cleared the air and had shared one of the best kisses he'd ever had, he didn't want to overstep again.

But he wanted to tell her to go for her dreams and study her music. He'd had countless moments where he'd been afraid to take a leap, whether it was applying to business school, putting together his business plan, or just having a difficult conversation with someone. And in those situations, other people had given him the little push he needed. Every single time, he'd found something satisfying and worth fighting for when he'd taken a leap of faith and pushed himself. He wanted to pass on what others had done for him and pay it forward.

"Okay," he murmured to himself. "Passion. Following your passion."

He cracked a few eggs into a bowl and whisked them as he tried to put the words together in a way that made sense. His emotions were getting in the way. He already cared about Hannah a lot and knew that she had the talent to make it with her music.

"Have you ever thought of pursuing your music outside of Blueberry Bay?" he said, trying the words on for size. "No, that's not good. Maybe starting with the passion piece?"

He pushed his diced vegetables around in his pan, running a hand through his hair in mild frustration. The moment he had the thoughts in order, they seemed to slip from his head.

"I should have started with coffee," he said to himself, turning the heat down and putting down his spatula to start a pot. "Need to get my thoughts in order."

He started the process, staring at the pot as it slowly filled. Just the smell of it woke his brain up and it came to him.

"Hannah, do you ever think about what your life would be like if you really dove into your passion?" Luke thought the words over. No, they still weren't right.

Some giggles behind him made him jump and turn around, his cheeks burning. Sandy was standing there in her pajamas, a smile on her face.

"What's up?" Sandy asked.

"Just cooking breakfast." Luke went back to the stove and poured the whisked eggs over the cooked vegetables.

"And talking to your food?"

"No." Luke laughed. "I want to go to The Crab and talk to Hannah about something important but I don't want to offend her. It's kind of big so I wanted to rehearse it before I put my foot in my mouth."

"Ah." Sandy went on her tiptoes and grabbed a mug from the cabinet. "Hannah's a sweet girl. I'm sure she won't be offended if you're kind and thoughtful. And I know you will be."

That made his shoulders release tension he hadn't realized he'd been holding. Sandy was right. He flipped the omelet onto a plate.

"Do you want an omelet?" he asked.

"No, I'm good." Sandy poured Luke a cup of coffee too. "What were you going to talk to Hannah about?"

"Have you heard her play the piano before?" Luke took his coffee and his food to the small table on the far side of the kitchen.

"I think so? Not in a long time." Sandy wandered in his direction, but didn't sit. "Is she still playing?"

"Yeah, she is. I stumbled upon her playing the piano at The Crab the other day. She's incredible. Super talented," Luke said. "I think she should follow her passion for it. Maybe go to school or something. I asked her about it and she said she hadn't really thought about it seriously. So maybe she just needs some encouragement. I know she can do it."

Sandy gave him a knowing smile and his cheeks warmed up. He hadn't hidden his crush on her whatsoever, had he? Then again, he didn't want to hide it now. They had kissed and he hoped that they could see where their feelings went.

"Just be honest and be yourself. Everything will work out just fine," Sandy said.

She gave him a side hug before going back to their home office. Luke dug into his omelet, his courage to talk to Hannah rising. Sandy was right. He just had to be himself and it would all be okay.

* * *

Hannah fell into the steady rhythm of wrapping up silverware behind the counter. The breakfast rush had died down, giving her the chance to breathe. She glanced up at the lingering customers, enjoying their breakfast sandwiches and iced coffee. Just as she looked back down at the silverware, the bell above the door chimed and Luke walked in.

Her heart did a flip in her chest twice, first at the sight of Luke, and the second at her surprise that seeing him made her have such a strong reaction. She smiled and gave him a shy wave, which he returned along with a lopsided smile. His smile made his whole face light up in a way that she adored.

"Hey," she said when he got to the counter, her cheeks warming. She wasn't sure what to do with her hands all of a sudden, so she tucked them into the pockets of the apron around her hips. "What's up?"

"Not much. How are you?"

"Good." Hannah bit her bottom lip, resisting the urge to fidget.

"You look really pretty today," he said, his voice shy.

Hannah didn't feel that way. Something about rushing around and handling a lot of greasy food made her feel rumpled at all times. And today she hadn't bothered with much makeup at all beyond some concealer and chapstick. But Luke was so earnest about it that she had to smile.

"Thank you," she said, her whole body heating up. "Can I get you anything?"

"Um..." Luke looked up at the menu, his expression lost. "What do you suggest?"

"Depends on what you're after. Something sweet? Something savory? Something big or something small?"

"Hm. Would it be weird to get a coffee and chocolate milkshake at this hour?" he asked.

"Nope, there's coffee in it." Hannah grinned and rang it up. "I'll have it ready in a second."

After Luke paid, she made the milkshake, the first of the day. She handed it over to him and watched him take his first sip.

"It's really good," he said. "I want to chug it but I'll get brain freeze."

"Yeah, it's all in the ice cream. We get it from a guy who has a dairy farm nearby."

Luke took another long sip despite just saying that he wanted to avoid brain freeze. "Do you have a second for a break? I wanted to talk to you about something."

"Yeah, sure." Hannah's heart soared up like a bird caught on a breeze. Did he want to talk about starting a relationship like she had been thinking about too?

They went to the long counter alongside the wall and sat next to each other, their knees only inches apart.

"So, what's up?" Hannah asked.

Luke took a deep breath before he spoke. "I don't want you to get offended by this or anything, but I wanted to run an idea by you."

Hannah's heart took a sharp dip downward. What could he have to tell her that was possibly going to offend her? "Okay, go for it."

"You're so talented on the piano, better than anyone I've ever heard who wasn't a pro," Luke said. "Have you ever thought about sending an audition video to a college to study music more seriously?"

Hannah blinked, unsure of what to say.

"My university has a school of music—Jacob's School of Music at Indiana University," he continued. "I think that you would be a great fit. They take rolling admissions so you could apply right now."

Hannah's mouth opened, then closed since she didn't know what to say. Playing the piano had always been a solitary thing for her. In some ways, she liked it that way. She had never performed for an audience before or even played with others around. The thought of being around people who were better than her made her heart pound. What if they judged her?

"I don't think I would be good enough. I've only taught myself," Hannah said.

Luke took her hand, which was slightly cooler than hers from holding onto his milkshake. The touch comforted her.

"You'll never know if you don't try. What's the worst that could happen? Them saying no?" He shrugged. "And I'm pretty sure that you're more than good enough anyway."

Hannah tried to slow down her breathing and take in what he was saying.

"But I don't know the first thing about recording an audition video," she stammered. "Don't I need special sound equipment and all that stuff?"

"Leave that up to me. I've got all the gadgets and gear you'll need." He squeezed her hand. "Will you do it?"

Hannah swallowed. He believed in her so much, and that made it easier for her to believe in herself.

"Yes. I'll try it," Hannah said. "Thank you for believing in me."

"It's no problem. Anyone who's heard you play would believe in you too." Luke smiled.

Hannah swung her legs back and forth, her heels

hitting the stool she was sitting on. As much she wanted to give this a shot, she wasn't making the decision in a vacuum. She looked over her shoulder at the kitchen, where her dad was cooking.

"I understand about your dad," Luke said, reading her mind. "But have you ever talked to him directly about it? I can't imagine that he'd be against you going for your passion."

Hannah took in a deep breath again. She hadn't ever brought this up with him, but she had to at some point. But bringing it up before she even recorded her video or got in sounded a bit premature.

"I'll talk to him if I get in," she said.

Luke smiled, and Hannah couldn't help but smile in return.

CHAPTER EIGHTEEN

Alissa sipped her coffee as she came into *The Outlet*'s office, ready for the upcoming week. Josie was at her desk as always, working away.

"Morning!" Alissa said.

"Good morning!" Josie smiled at her before going back to what she was working on.

Alissa went past her to Dane's office to say hello, but she found his office empty. She checked her watch. It was a little past nine and Dane was almost always in. Maybe he was going on a quick coffee run. But then again, she would have run into him on her way to the office since she had also grabbed something on the way.

She put her bag down and went over to Josie's desk.

"Where's Dane?" Alissa asked.

"He took the day off today."

"What?" Alissa hadn't meant to raise her voice, but she was shocked. "Dane? Taking a day off?"

"Yeah." Josie shrugged. "I was surprised too."

Alissa frowned and looked back at his office. Was he sick? He would have told her if he was. Maybe he had something to do.

"Weird," Alissa murmured before going back to her office.

When she sat down, she noticed a folded piece of paper sticking up in her keyboard. She unfolded it and found a note from Dane. All it said was for her to meet him at The Crab around sunset. Her brows furrowed and she flipped the paper over to see if there was any more information. Nothing.

"What are you up to, Dane?" she murmured to herself, her heart pounding out of her chest.

What was this about? Was it a bad thing? He had just been so sweet and romantic before. Had he somehow changed his mind?

She opened up her email and her latest article, but couldn't focus on them or anything else for the rest of the day.

* * *

Dane paced across the deck of The Crab, adjusting the grass skirt that he'd put along the edge of one of the tables. He and Hannah had decorated the area for Dane's surprise for Alissa, making it like a mini luau before the actual event. His hands were so sweaty that they stuck to the fabric hibiscus flowers in a vase. He was worried he was going to knock over one of the many candles they'd lit and catch the whole thing on fire.

He glanced over his shoulder toward where the rest of the restaurant's tables were. Even though he wanted to surprise Alissa with what he'd learned, he didn't want half of Blueberry Bay to witness it too. Not just because he was shy—though he had the moves down by heart now—but because he wanted it to just be for her. He hoped she'd love it.

"We're good," Hannah said, accurately reading his mind. "I promise everyone will be seated over there so your moment won't be ruined."

"Good. Thanks." He blew out a breath and adjusted his printed shirt. It was way more flashy than anything he'd ever wear—dark blue with green and white printed hibiscus flowers on it. "I think it looks good."

"It does. Oh, and I have the luau music good to

go for when Alissa shows up," Hannah said, standing with her hands on her hips.

Dane took another deep breath, making Hannah laugh.

"What?" Dane asked.

"You look like you're going on your first date. Like not just your first date with Alissa, but your first date, period," Hannah said.

Dane had to crack a smile at that. "I kind of do feel like that. I've never done anything like this for anyone. I feel like I know the steps but what if I forget and make a fool of myself?"

Hannah's expression softened. "Genuine effort and caring about another person's feelings can't be taken wrong," she said. "I'm sure she'll be excited no matter what."

Dane rolled his shoulders back, consciously keeping the tension out of them. Hannah was right. Even if Alissa only saw the decorations, she'd be happy.

"Oh, here she comes!" Hannah whispered, rushing over to her phone, which was hooked up to Bluetooth speakers.

Dane swallowed and got into position, his heart racing even though it was just them. Alissa rounded the corner and stopped the moment she took in the scene. Hula music started playing and Dane started the dance.

He was nervous at first, fumbling his hands, but once he recovered, his muscle memory took him through the moves. Alissa stood with one hand limp by her side and the other clutching the strap of her bag. The disbelief on her face made Dane bolder and he danced toward her.

He slid his arm around her waist and pulled her closer. Her grin spread across her face and her eyes shined with unshed tears.

"Dane..." She looked around the scene he and Hannah had set up, taking in the leis and all of the candles. "Is this what you've been working on? The dancing?"

"Yes." Dane guided them through a few steps, turning them around. "For a while now."

"After work? All those meetings with Josie?"

"Every one of those." The music slowed and he stopped them, still holding her close.

"Wow." Alissa dabbed at her eyes underneath her glasses. "I was afraid you and Josie were interested in each other or something."

"Oh, definitely not." Dane snorted. "She offered to help me learn how to do the hula so I wouldn't embarrass you at the luau. She's taken dance lessons and really helped me break down the steps."

Alissa grinned. "I don't think you'd embarrass me."

"You didn't see me almost fall flat on my face when I first started learning," he said. "So I'm glad I prepared. I'm trying my best to embrace life here and be a little less serious. I hope this is a good step in that direction."

Alissa pulled him closer so they were hugging and held him there for several moments. The familiar fruity scent of her shampoo warmed Dane from the inside out. He heard her sniff, like she was crying, so Dane pulled back. She wasn't crying, but she was clearly overwhelmed.

"This is incredible, Dane. Thank you," Alissa said.

"It's no problem." Dane kissed her on the forehead. "And finally, I can ask you—would you like to go to the luau with me?"

Alissa beamed. "I'd love to."

They kissed, and Dane felt Alissa's smile the entire time.

CHAPTER NINETEEN

Hannah pulled up to Sandy and Daniel's house, her stomach in knots. She had gotten off work early so she could record her audition video, telling her dad that she had some errands to run. Luke had gotten off early too to help her record.

She'd practiced every night, making sure she had every last piece down forward and backward, especially the one that the school of music required her to play. Still, her hands were so sweaty that she was worried her fingers were going to slip on the keys.

She got out when she saw Luke come out the front door, waving.

"Hey," Luke said with a smile.

"Hi." The same fluttery feeling she got whenever she saw Luke mingled with her nervous stomach.

"You ready?" Luke pushed the front door open for her.

"I'm ridiculously nervous but I'm here. So I guess?" Hannah shrugged as they rounded the corner to where Sandy and Daniel's piano sat.

"You'll be great. Once you warm up a little, I'm sure it'll feel like you've been playing on this piano for ages," Luke said, resting his hand on her upper back.

The warmth of his big hand slowed the nervous butterflies threatening to overtake her whole body.

"Yeah?" Hannah asked.

"I'm sure of it." He showed her the piano. "Here it is. Sandy said they had it tuned recently, so it should be in perfect shape."

Hannah ran her fingers along the keys. It was a lovely piano, simple but solid. And it was a similar size and shape as the one she played at The Crab, which brought her nerves down even more. She sat down at the bench, making a fist and releasing it several times to stretch out her hands. She played a chord, just to try it out—the weight of the keys, the tone of it. It felt familiar right away.

"It does sound good." Hannah grinned, playing some scales to warm up.

"Good, because I've got the best equipment to capture the sound as accurately as possible," Luke said, going over to the camera on a tripod a few feet away. "And I have this microphone."

He disappeared into the other room for a moment and returned with a microphone on a stand. It was taller than him and hung above the piano when he placed it next to it.

"Want to do a little bit of test playing?" Luke asked. "Just so we can see how it sounds?"

"Sure. I'll keep playing these scales, I guess. Keep warming up."

Luke went behind the camera and hit record. Being recorded changed things, making her feel tense and awkward in her skin. She had gone home to change into something a little nicer and had done her hair and makeup, but suddenly it didn't feel right.

"You okay?" Luke asked.

"Yeah." Hannah sighed, tucking her hair behind her ear. "Just feeling self-conscious when the camera's rolling."

"Ah, that makes sense. Let me stop for a

moment." Luke hit pause on the recording and came around to her. "You want to take a second?"

"Sure." She let her hands fall into her lap and sighed. "I'm not sure what's wrong. I felt fine just a second ago. I think I got in my own head about how I look. I've never seen myself playing piano before and I'm worried I'll look stupid."

"You look beautiful and you look amazing when you play," Luke said. "You're so into it that it's hard to *not* watch you."

"Really?" Hannah straightened up.

"Yeah. Keep doing your warmups for as long as you need. And we can do as many takes as you need."

Hannah smiled, smoothing her hands down her pants. "If you ever decide to skip your career in tech repair, you'd be an amazing motivational speaker."

They both laughed. Hannah started to play again, going through her scales and a few warmup songs. Luke's encouragement had boosted her confidence, and the familiar scales made her even more comfortable.

"Okay," Hannah said, squeezing her knees. "I'm ready to start."

"All right." Luke went behind the camera again. "I'll press record on three."

Luke counted down and hit record. Hannah froze for a beat, but started to play her piece. It was the one that Luke had heard when he ran into her at The Crab, though she had changed it. The beginning started off melancholy, soft and haunting, but eventually it grew into something hopeful.

Hannah slipped into the music, letting the notes she'd created and practiced again and again flow out of her. Her body moved as she played, emphasizing the notes that she wanted to bring out. She lost track of herself as the song shifted into its upbeat ending, a smile spreading across her face. She finished with a flourish and sat back, resting her hands on her knees.

Luke was grinning from ear to ear and stopped the recording, the red light above it turning off.

"That was incredible, Hannah," Luke said. "I loved it."

"Thank you. I think I nailed it." She ran her finger down the keys from the lowest notes to the highest. "But can we record another take, just in case? Before we record the other songs?"

"Sure thing."

They recorded another take, which was just as perfect as the first, and went on to the other songs that Hannah had to record for her audition. She ended with the song the school required everyone to play, a big smile on her face.

It all felt so real now, like she could actually imagine herself moving away and expanding on her skills. When Luke showed her the footage back, her dream became so vivid she could almost see it right in front of her.

"Thank you again for all of your help and encouragement, Luke," Hannah said, closing the cover over the keys. "I couldn't have done this without you."

"It's not a problem at all. This was great." He tucked his hands into the front pockets of his jeans. "Can I ask you something?"

Her stomach flip-flopped in her belly. This experience had made her feel so much closer to him. Did he feel the same way?

"Shoot."

"Do you want to go to the luau with me?" His cheeks above his beard were flushed, which Hannah found almost unbearably endearing.

"Of course, I'd love to." Hannah's smile turned sheepish. "I thought you were going to ask me to date you."

Luke's eyes widened. "Oh."

"Sorry!" Hannah held up her hands, waving

them as if to clear the air. "I was being way too forward."

"No, don't apologize," he said, resting a hand on her upper arm. "I'm just surprised because I was thinking the same thing but I didn't want to be too pushy. Here I am, encouraging you to do this already."

"You aren't too pushy at all. I'm glad we're on the same wavelength." Hannah's expression softened. "I'm not sure how things will work out between my audition and maybe moving away from here, but I do know I like you a lot. And there's still time this summer to get to know each other more."

Luke slid his hand down her arm until they were holding hands. "Yeah, we have plenty of time. I want to get to know you better too."

They smiled at each other, and Luke leaned in to give her a soft kiss on the cheek. The simple gesture filled Hannah with excitement. She couldn't wait for the luau or for the rest of the summer. It was going to be the best one yet.

CHAPTER TWENTY

Caitlin sighed, looking around the living room. She had been packing everything up in boxes in preparation for moving out. James had taken Pearl out to the zoo to give her time to do some packing, so the house felt emptier than it ever had.

They had started the paperwork for their separation, but they hadn't figured out all the details of their divorce yet. And there were so many details. Lawyers. Pearl. The restaurant and all of the paperwork that went with owning it.

But she felt a tiny flutter in her stomach. Things were changing and she was nervous, but she had to keep moving forward.

She picked up a photo of Pearl at a dance recital that they had framed and placed on the mantel above the fireplace. It was a favorite of both her and James, so she left it in place. They'd figure out who got this particular frame and photo later.

She worked through the living room, grabbing the things that were one hundred percent hers and wrapping them in paper or bubble wrap. The more she packed, the more she realized how much she had put into this house—the decorations, the furniture, all of it.

Neither she or James had any idea what they were going to do about the house. James wanted an apartment closer to the restaurant and Caitlin wanted whatever worked best.

An apartment, or maybe a rental in a house somewhere? She wasn't sure. She and James had been together so long that she forgot what it was like to have a space be primarily hers. She needed a room for Pearl, of course, but she'd have full reign over most of the space.

Caitlin wiped sweat off her forehead with the back of her hand and sat down on the couch. She deserved a break.

She pulled her phone from the pocket of her leggings and called Alissa.

"Hey," Alissa said, sounding slightly out of breath.

"Hey. Did I catch you at a bad time?"

"No, I just had to run to my phone and I've been rushing around with the luau coming up," Alissa said. "I definitely need a break."

"Oh, good. I'm taking a break too." Caitlin looked around the living room. She needed to make a path so no one would trip on the boxes.

"Packing?"

"Yep. I'm working on the living room," she said.

"Are you doing okay?" Alissa asked, her voice gentle. "Holding up?"

"As much as I can, yeah." Caitlin pushed her hair out of her face. "It's been weird. I don't know how to feel, really. One minute I'm sad looking at a piece of furniture that we picked out together, then the next I'm shocked that this is actually happening, then the next I'm just relieved."

"That's totally understandable. How's Pearl doing?"

Caitlin absently rubbed her chest, which ached at the memory of telling Pearl that they were getting divorced. She was upset and confused, but she and James had emphasized that it wasn't because of her and that they loved her very much.

"She's doing okay, I think." Caitlin nibbled on her bottom lip. "She hasn't been acting out or anything, but sometimes I wonder if she's hiding it."

"I'm sure she'll talk to you about it if she needs to. You two are close," Alissa said.

The reassurance from Alissa boosted Caitlin's confidence.

"I hope this is the right move in the long run for her too." Caitlin grabbed a throw pillow to hold onto. "It might be hard sometimes but I think it'll be better than growing up in a home where her parents don't really love each other or even see eye to eye."

"Good point. And you guys will co-parent too so you both will be in her life," Alissa added. "I know you'll all make it through once the hardest parts of this are over."

"Yeah, exactly." Caitlin smiled. Even though they were wildly different, Alissa truly got her. "How are things with Dane?"

"They're great! All of those meetings were just a misunderstanding," Alissa said.

"Oh? How?"

"He was learning how to hula dance for me." The delight in Alissa's voice warmed Caitlin's heart.

"Dane? Dancing?" Caitlin had to laugh, but covered her mouth. "I can't imagine that. He's loosened up but dancing?"

"I know! He was good too." Alissa laughed too. "He set up this whole surprise at The Crab where he danced for me and decorated everything like we were having our own mini-luau. And then he asked me to it, finally. So all of those nights he was at the office late, he was preparing all of this."

"That's so sweet," Caitlin said, her heart warming. "I'm glad it all worked out for you two."

Hearing Alissa's story had really made her day. It gave her the hope that she really needed in that moment. Somewhere out there was a man who'd do something like that for her, even if it wasn't the man she was about to divorce. Love was real.

"Thanks."

"I really need to come to Blueberry Bay soon," Caitlin said, propping her feet up on the coffee table. "I definitely need some fresh sea air and sunshine."

"You definitely should. It's gorgeous right now. Warm, but the breeze really helps," Alissa said. "You and Pearl should come! Pearl would love it here. Maybe you could stay for a little while."

Caitlin smiled. "I love that idea. And Pearl would love it too."

* * *

The warm, salty breeze coming in from the water made it all the way to *The Outlet*'s offices, coming through the windows that Alissa had thrown open earlier. It added to the atmosphere the luau was spreading across the entire town. Businesses were decorating their windows and doors, and some were even playing music.

Alissa had decorated the inside of the office already, but the outside was still looking plain. She and Josie had armfuls of streamers, flower-shaped string lights, and leis to make the outside just as festive as the inside.

"Could you hand me a little more tape, please?" Alissa asked Josie. "These streamers might fall in the breeze."

"Sure thing." Josie handed her the tape from her spot next to Alissa's ladder.

Alissa secured the streamers above the door and hopped off the ladder to take a look. It was bright and colorful, but it still needed more.

"Ready for the lights?" Alissa asked, picking up the box. She pulled them out, stretching the wire between them. "These are so cute. I'm glad you found them."

Each light was shaped like a hibiscus flower in a different color. Once they were on, they would match the streamers and make all the other decorations more eye-catching.

"They were a steal too." Josie took one end of the lights and helped Alissa pull them out. "That website I found seriously helped."

Alissa wasn't surprised that Josie had found something like this. She was great at solving almost any problem thrown her way.

Alissa got up on the ladder again, a removable hook in hand. She looked over her shoulder at Josie as she positioned it, a question in her eyes.

"It's a little uneven. Can you lift it a little higher?" Josie stepped back to get a better look.

"Like this?" Alissa lifted the hook.

"Perfect."

Alissa pressed it into place, then did the same on the other side of the door. They had to wait for a few minutes for the adhesive to cure, so they stepped back toward the parking lot to take the whole scene in. Alissa was almost sad that they'd have to take it all down eventually, but she pushed that thought aside. She didn't have to think about it ending—she could enjoy it right now while it lasted.

"I'm so excited," Alissa said. "Thank you for helping Dane with his dance moves. The way he showed me was so sweet and perfect."

The memory still made her heart flutter. After he finished showing off his moves, they ate dinner together, a preview of the Hawaiian burger that The Crab was going to serve during the luau. It was delicious and Alissa couldn't wait to have another one. They had talked late into the evening until Hannah started to close out the restaurant. After, they'd walked on the beach holding hands until they were both too sleepy to continue.

"That's what he was hoping for. I was happy to help him out." Josie grinned. "He worked so hard on getting it right."

"He did an amazing job." Alissa tucked her hands into the pockets of her linen t-shirt dress. "I was a little concerned, though. But it was all worth it in the end."

"I'm happy to hear it."

They stood in comfortable silence for a few moments, which Alissa savored. She almost felt silly for worrying about whether Dane and Josie were involved. Josie was becoming one of her good friends. She wouldn't have done anything to hurt her or Dane.

"Speaking of the luau, are you going with anyone?"

"Nope, just me." Josie shrugged. "Everyone's

going, so I'm sure I'll find people to hang out with. You and Dane included."

"Michael is available." Alissa gently nudged Josie with her elbow and smiled.

Josie laughed, playing with the charm bracelet she was wearing. "Thanks, but no thanks. I'm fine being single for now. The luau will be fun either way."

Alissa grinned, the future bright ahead of her. "Yeah, it will be."

* * *

Hannah tossed another dress onto her bed and sighed. Most of her clothes were functional—jeans, t-shirts, leggings—but she had dresses and skirts in the depths of her closet. Apparently they were very, very deep in her closet, but she knew they were there. One of them had to be perfect for the luau, but she wasn't sure which one was the best.

She looked over her shoulder at the mountain of clothes on her bed. At least fifty percent of them were jeans or leggings.

"I really need to pare down on pants," she murmured to herself, going back into her closet.

She found a light blue dress that she forgot she

had and changed into it. The second she shifted the skirt and the neckline into place, she remembered why it had languished in the back of her closet for over a year—it rode up in the back, the zipper never laid flat, and the tag itched even after she cut it out as close to the seam as possible.

Instead of tossing it back into her closet, she grabbed a garbage bag from the kitchen, wrote "donate" on a piece of masking tape, and stuffed the dress in there. She figured she might as well multitask if she was emptying out her closet.

She dug through her closet more and tried on a few more dresses. Some still fit, but weren't festive enough, but others went straight into the donation bin. Then, she found the perfect outfit—a long blue skirt and a white off-the-shoulder blouse. She put it on and looked at herself in the mirror. It was perfectly beachy and comfortable, and would fit the theme perfectly once she did her hair.

She sat down at her small vanity and tugged her ponytail holder out of her hair. After finger combing it, she pushed it around, trying to decide what the best look was. Simple was better—down, with a flower. But which one? She had brought a few leftover fabric flower decorations home from The Crab, which she held up to her head. The flower looked best on the side of her hair, but it wouldn't stay if she just tucked it there. It would be perfect once she stuck the flower to a hair pin with hot glue so she wouldn't have to worry about the wind blowing it away.

Someone tapped on her bedroom door, opening up a crack.

"Come in!" Hannah said.

Willis pushed the door open all the way and smiled when he took Hannah in.

"You look beautiful. Picking out an outfit for the luau?" He leaned against her door frame.

"Thanks. And yeah, I am." She held up a pink flower and an orange flower. "Which color?"

"Oh, hmm." Willis ran his hand through his hair and let out a chuckle. "Whichever you want."

Hannah grinned. Her dad was far from fashionable, not that he had to be. He dressed for function, wearing the same old jeans, sneakers, and flannel shirts that he'd worn for ages.

"Okay, I'll make both into hair clips and go from there." Hannah put the flowers down, smoothing her hands down her skirt. They were slightly damp from sweat. "Can I ask you something?"

"Go ahead."

"Is it really okay if I start seeing Luke?" she

asked. "Because I think I want to even though I don't know what'll happen after this summer. He definitely won't be staying here."

Willis came further into her room and sat on the edge of her bed. "Well, does he make you happy?"

"Yeah." The fluttery feeling she got whenever she thought of him appeared. "He's great."

"And he's a good guy." Willis shrugged. "I'm just glad to see you happy, so of course you should date him. Do whatever feels best in your heart."

A lump appeared in Hannah's throat, but she swallowed it before it led to her tearing up. Why had she worried about asking her father about this? He loved her and only wanted her to be happy no matter what.

Her thoughts went to the audition tape she'd sent in. What would he think if she got accepted? Would he be as caring as he was now? She wasn't sure, and she had no idea what she was going to do if she got in.

CHAPTER TWENTY-ONE

Dane swallowed, his heart pounding as he pulled up outside of Alissa's place. He had planned surprise dates in the past—nice dinners, outings to Boston to see museum exhibits, things of that sort. But this date was the biggest yet. He'd woken up in a cold sweat about it.

Today was their very first surfing lesson.

His worry wasn't that Alissa would hate it—no, he had the feeling she was going to be delighted. She had talked about learning how to surf off and on ever since they went to their first surfing competition together back in the winter, and it popped up more and more as the weather warmed.

But he was utterly and completely terrified. He took a deep breath and let it out as he texted Alissa to let her know he had arrived. Everything outside of his comfort zone was going to be scary. This just happened to be a huge step. A leap into the unknown.

Alissa came outside in her swimsuit cover-up, sunglasses on. All he had told her was that they were going to be near the water and that she should dress accordingly. She grinned, sliding into the passenger seat and planting a kiss on his cheek.

"Hey," Alissa said. "I'm excited for whatever this is."

"You should be." Dane put his car into drive and headed toward the water.

"You're not going to give me a single hint as to what it is, are you?"

"Nope, because that would ruin the surprise." Dane smiled.

"Ugh, I love and hate surprises." Alissa sighed. "Can you give me a –"

"No hints. Being near the water is enough of one."

Alissa playfully glared at him. "Okay, fine, I'll play along. Is it another boat ride?"

Dane snorted. "You just said you were going to play along with the surprise, then you ask what it is?"

Alissa waved her hand and looked out the

window, her grin widening. "I'm just trying to keep you on your toes."

"You do that anyway."

Dane held Alissa's hand over the car console the rest of the drive and parked in the lot next to the beach. It was filled with cars, so they were farther away. But that was perfect—it built up more and more anticipation. He took Alissa's hand and guided her down toward the water.

When Alissa finally realized where they were going, she gasped and clasped his arm.

"You're kidding," Alissa said. "Dane..."

"I'm not." Dane pulled her closer. "We're going to learn how to surf."

Alissa stopped, pulling Dane into a huge hug. Dane wrapped his arms around her and held her close.

"I can't believe you set this up. I'm so excited." She released him. "You're doing it with me?"

"Yep, I am."

Alissa's grin was worth whatever embarrassing or potentially uncomfortable things he was about to experience.

The class was gathered near the edge of the water, where two instructors were starting to help people put on wet suits and pick out boards. One was a young man with a buzz cut and a dimpled smile, who noticed them first.

"Hey there!" he said. "Here for the surfing lesson?"

"Yes, we are," Dane replied, hoping his nerves didn't show as much as he felt them. "We're Dane and Alissa."

"Awesome. My name is Tyler and that's Bee. We're your instructors today. Let's get you guys set up with some wet suits and boards."

Dane went with Tyler and Bee went with Alissa. Alissa was right—the wetsuit did cover most of his skin, though he'd slathered on a bunch of sunscreen before he left. Next came the board, which was a simple foam one, and holding onto it made his stomach flip upside down.

They lined up in front of Bee and Tyler once the other four people in the class had been outfitted too.

"Okay, we're ready to start!" Bee clapped her hands together. Her brown hair was already damp, as if she'd caught some waves before teaching class. "We're going to start on land before we even think about getting in the water."

Dane's shoulders relaxed. The land he could handle. And maybe it would help him be less worried about getting into the water. He glanced over at Alissa as Bee and Tyler explained the basics of safety and the rules they had to follow during the lessons. She was listening intently, her eyes bright.

Seeing how much she was into it calmed his nerves a bit. As long as she was by his side, it would be okay.

Tyler and Bee demonstrated the proper paddling technique, which Dane and Alissa got the hang of, but the technique of hopping up on the board was another story. Dane considered himself in decent shape, but the simple act of going from his stomach to his feet had him huffing and puffing.

But it was exhilarating at the same time—the sand, the water, the feeling of the ocean air coming into his lungs. Most of his worries were starting to fade away as he took in the moment. Well, in between hopping up and down on his board.

"At least we'll be getting in the water soon," Alissa said, trying to catch her breath after yet another drill. "To cool down."

"True, but then we'll be doing all this while wet." Dane rested his hands on his hips, trying to slow his breathing.

He looked out onto the water. The waves here were small, far from the big, intimidating ones that he saw the professional surfers on during the competitions. Of course that was the case, but in his anxious dreams, he'd been swallowed up in crashing tides before he could even think about hopping up on his board.

"Okay, I think you guys are ready to start trying some small waves. Let's space out some. Everyone to my right, go with Tyler. Everyone else, come with me." Bee gestured to the two sides of the group.

Luckily Dane and Alissa were in the same group —Tyler's. Dane's heart started to race again as they waded through the water, their boards alongside them, until they were waist deep. This was it. All of his fears came rushing back—falling off his board, making a fool of himself, not being able to even get up on the board at all.

He took a deep breath and focused on Alissa walking beside him. He could do this for her. He was already halfway there anyway. Like with his hula dance practice, everything had a learning curve. Just because he failed the first few times didn't mean he was doomed to fail forever. Plus, he wasn't the only beginner.

If he'd learned anything from learning to dance, he learned that he had to throw himself into these situations and think about how to swim later. He always figured it out.

The third person in their group went first, a thirty-something woman with her hair slicked back into a ballerina's bun. She hopped up with the grace of a dancer, but lost balance soon after she got to her feet. Next came Alissa. Her lovely features were fixed in concentration as she paddled, hoisting herself up onto the board. She made it halfway up before falling off into the water.

"You're up, Dane," Tyler said from where he was standing.

Dane swallowed and got into position. The rocking of the water made the board that had obviously felt so stable on land feel completely foreign. Alissa gave him a thumbs up, so clearly excited for him that she boosted his confidence.

He paddled, the swell of the water buoying him upward. When he felt the point that Tyler had noted, Dane tried to get up on the board. His balance was completely off and he flopped into the ocean. The water wasn't too deep, so falling in wasn't nearly as bad as he thought it would be.

Alissa, Tyler, and the other member of their group cheered for him regardless. He pushed his hair out of his face and paddled back to the others.

"That wasn't so bad, was it?" Alissa said.

"It really wasn't," Dane replied.

"It'll only get better from here. Let's keep trying," Tyler said.

They kept taking turns, most of them not managing to get to their feet. When Alissa did, they all cheered. The look on her face as she rode her wave was priceless —she could have lit up half the beach with her smile.

"You're up again, Dane." Tyler gestured toward the waves.

Something in Dane's gut told him that this was the one—he was going to properly surf this next wave. He felt the movement of the water underneath his board, shifting his weight to balance. Something between him and the powerful ocean below clicked.

He got to his feet, found his balance, and *surfed*. Not for long, and it probably didn't look impressive, but the feeling was so enthralling that he wondered why he'd ever hesitated to embrace even the scarier things that Blueberry Bay had to offer.

When he came down, the entire class was cheering for him. Dane couldn't wipe the smile off his face, pride making his heart grow. He pulled Alissa into a quick kiss when he got back to where the rest of the group was waiting.

"Thank you for setting this up," she said, resting her head against his shoulder. "It's been amazing."

"Thank you for showing me how much fun there is outside of my comfort zone." He kissed the top of her damp head. "I can't wait to keep trying new things."

* * *

Luke knelt down to reorganize a shelf of candy that two little kids had ransacked not long ago. The foot traffic into the store had been picking up with the luau happening the next day, so he'd spent most of the day on his feet, restocking shelves, pointing customers in the right direction, and cleaning up messes.

Once the candy shelf was back in order, he went to the front of the store. Sandy was ringing up a customer's order and Daniel was chatting with a regular customer about the luau.

"Need any help up here?" Luke asked Sandy.

"Nope, I'm good." Sandy smiled. "Have you taken a break this afternoon?"

Luke checked his watch, his eyes widening. "I didn't realize time had gone by this fast. I haven't taken a proper break yet since things keep popping up."

"Take one whenever you'd like. We've got it under control up here."

Luke debated what to do on his break. Some days he took a walk and other days he read a book down by the water. But a glimpse at the mailman, who had just walked through the door, changed his plans entirely. He had a stack of mail sticking out of his bag, the red and white insignia of Indiana University on a big white envelope jumping out at him.

His heart pounded in his chest as he got closer and saw the Jacob's School of Music's name on it as well. Without thinking, he snatched the letter up and checked if it was real. Hannah's name was on it. His hands trembled as if the letter were for himself. This envelope held Hannah's future in it—all of the things that she hoped for and he hoped for for her were going to be revealed in a very short time.

He looked up, feeling multiple sets of eyes on him, including the mailman's.

"I... can I see this letter?" Luke asked the mailman, giving him a sheepish look as he held up the envelope.

"Uh, sure. This is for The Crab, though?" The mailman still looked extremely confused, and Luke didn't blame him. He was whipped into a frenzy for mail that wasn't even his.

"What's going on?" Sandy asked, craning her neck to see what the commotion was.

"Is everything okay?" Daniel's brows furrowed.

"Yeah. It's just that it's news from IU for Hannah. About her audition for the music school." Luke held it up. "Can I take their mail to them?"

"Sure. Here's the rest of it." The mailman handed Luke a small stack of mail. Luke tucked it behind the envelope from Indiana University.

"Thanks!"

Luke rushed off, jogging for a few moments before breaking into a run. People turned to look at him in confusion, but that didn't slow him down. He had to get to Hannah.

He burst into The Crab and spotted Hannah serving a table, a big smile on her face. Even though he was itching to burst toward her and tell her the news, he waited until she was done with the table before striding to her side.

"Oh, hey, Luke!" Hannah said.

"Come with me." Luke took her hand and walked her toward the back.

"Wait, what? Why?" Hannah held on, putting

down her tray as she passed by the counter. "What's going on?"

Luke waited until they were in the back to pull the envelope from under his arm. Hannah rested her hand on the wall, her face going white in an instant.

"Is it..." She tentatively reached for the envelope, her hand inches from it like it was a hot pan on a stove.

"It is."

Hannah pressed one hand to her forehead and the other to her stomach, like she felt ill. "Luke, I don't know what to say. Or what to do."

"Open it, of course."

"I know but..." Hannah took a deep, shuddering breath. "It's a lot. I hardly knew I wanted to do this a few months ago and now I really, really want it."

"No matter what happens, you're still ridiculously talented," Luke said softly. "Open it."

Hannah reached for the envelope again before pulling her hand back. "No, I can't do it. Can you open it?"

"Sure." Luke slid his thumb under the envelope's seal, dragging it across.

Hannah had turned her back, pacing around with her hands on her hips. Luke's fingers trembled as he pulled the letter and the folder tucked inside from the envelope. His eyes went straight to the first sentences.

Dear Ms. Jenkins, we are pleased to inform you that...

"You got in!" Luke said, reading down the page. "With a scholarship!"

"Wait. What?" Hannah whipped around and grabbed the letter from him. Her eyes widened as she read it, looking between him and the paper as if she didn't think it was real. "Luke. I... I got in."

She threw her arms around him so hard that Luke nearly fell backward, but he stayed upright. He hugged her back, the smile on his face so broad that it almost hurt. Hannah eventually let him go and looked back at the letter. But this time, her expression was more torn.

"What's up?" Luke asked. "Are you not excited anymore?"

"No, I'm completely excited about this." Hannah held up the letter and the folder describing the program. "But I don't know how I'm going to tell my dad."

* * *

Hannah's mood had been a rollercoaster the entire day. One second, she was elated knowing that she had gotten in *and* gotten a scholarship. But the next, the thought of telling her father about it sent her into a spiral of doubt and anxiety.

She glanced at her father in the kitchen as he cleaned up in the kitchen for the day. They usually switched off closing in the back, and today was his day. She whipped through cleaning the restaurant in a nervous frenzy and now had time to think.

Still, she didn't know how to tell her dad about it all. All she knew was that she wanted to take the leap and try something new.

She straightened up a stack of cups for the third time before she wandered over to the piano to distract herself. Skimming her fingers along the keys relaxed her a little bit, and playing the beginning of an old jazz song she'd known for ages made the tension seep out of her even more. She slipped into the music, the smooth flow of it sweeping her away.

She had no idea how long she had been playing by the time Willis appeared at her side, watching her play with a smile on his face. The awe and love in his eyes made a lump appear in Hannah's throat. She wrapped up the piece she was playing and rested her hands in her lap.

"You're so amazing and talented, Hannah," Willis said.

Hannah had a grip on her emotions before, but her father's words blew down all of her defenses in an instant. She hiccupped and tears started falling from her eyes before she knew it. It was like she was so overwhelmed with the feelings inside of her that they spilled out in a flood. Willis came closer to her, resting a hand on her shoulder.

"Han, why are you crying?" Willis asked.

Hannah wiped her eyes and slid over so there was room for him on the piano bench. He sat down, putting an arm around her and pulling her into a side-hug.

It took Hannah a few moments, but Hannah gathered herself. She had to tell him—she couldn't put it off any longer.

"So, remember that evening I took off of work and said I had something to do with a friend?" Hannah asked. Willis frowned, then nodded. "I was at Sandy and Daniel's house with Luke, recording an audition video for the music school at Indiana University. And I just got a letter saying that I got in with a scholarship."

"Oh, Hannah, wow." Willis put his other arm around his daughter, holding her tight. "That's incredible! Do you not want to go? Is that why you're crying?"

"Wait, you're not upset?" Hannah sniffed, rubbing at her eyes again.

"Why would I be? That's amazing news. I'm so proud of you." Willis rubbed her back in slow circles the way he always did when she was overwhelmed.

"It's just... it's in Indiana. I have to leave Blueberry Bay and you and The Crab..." Hannah sighed. "Will you be okay without me? I don't want to leave everything to you or make life harder."

"I'll miss you, but it would hurt me more if I knew I was keeping you from following your dreams," he said, kissing the top of her head.

The weight lifted off of Hannah's chest, and any fog hiding her view of the future cleared away. She couldn't wait to see what this next stage in her life would bring her.

CHAPTER TWENTY-TWO

Finally, the day of the luau had arrived and Alissa was almost overwhelmed with her excitement. After writing about it for what felt like ages, she knew the event in and out. On one hand, it was great—she knew exactly where to go for what, and which activities and vendors she wanted to go to first. But on the other hand, she almost had *too* many options.

"Where do you want to go first?" Dane asked her, squeezing her hand.

"I don't know. We have so many options!"

She looked around the beach, where the center of the party was. To her right was the stage, where a few bands from the area were going to play some traditional Hawaiian music mixed with some fun crowd-pleasers. The first band was setting up already, testing the sound. Near them was a dance floor, where they were going to hula dance.

Games, themed activities, surfing, and a sandcastle contest were closer to the water, with groups of people already into the games. The vendors rounded it out on the far side of beach, the scents of more food than Alissa could possibly taste in one day drifting toward her when the breeze blew in the right way.

The whole beach was decorated beautifully too, with flowers, tiki torches, plants, and wooden masks peppered around the space, highlighting whatever activity was in a particular spot.

When she took a closer look, she saw her friends and people she had gotten to know since she moved to Blueberry Bay. Hannah and Willis were at The Crab's booth, which was already busy. Michael was down near the water with his surfboard, giving a demonstration. Tidal Wave Coffee's booth was running smoothly without him, serving up iced lattes and other coffee drinks made with macadamia nut milk and coconut milk. They even had a big sign advertising a boozy coffee drink that came in a fun mug.

"What about food first? Maybe a drink while we wander around?" Dane asked.

"Sure, that sounds good."

Dane led her through the crowd, saying hello to people and looking right at home in his Hawaiian shirt and shorts. She smiled, taking in the back of his head as he guided them. All of his efforts to embrace the town were starting to pay off. He fit in seamlessly.

The way he had embraced Blueberry Bay wasn't just good for him—it was going to work out wonderfully for the magazine, newspaper, and their lives together. He understood the people here and how the pace was slower, but that wasn't a bad thing. It was just his way of life now.

They arrived at the bar, which was appropriately placed toward the entrance of the food area, and got in line. The drinks were also on-theme, but Alissa couldn't decide what she wanted. The Blue Hawaii sounded good, though she'd never had one before, but so did the mai tai.

"What are you getting?" Dane asked. "I have no idea what I want, honestly."

"I'm torn between the Blue Hawaii and the mai tai. Maybe each of us could get one and we could taste each other's?" Alissa suggested.

"Sure, let's do that."

They got to the front of the line and ordered

their drinks. Alissa picked up the Blue Hawaii, its ocean blue color and little umbrella calling her name. She took a sip as they wandered away from the bar, lighting up. It was fruity and refreshing, just the right thing for the warm day. From the way Dane nodded, stirring his drink with his straw, he was pleased with it too.

"Oh, that's really good," Alissa said. "Taste!"

They swapped drinks and Alissa took the mai tai. It was just as good as the Blue Hawaii, sweet without being too cloying.

"We picked well." Dane smiled and took his mai tai back. "We can always loop back around and get more."

"True." Alissa leaned over and took one more sip of the mai tai through the straw, even as Dane held it. "Let's track down food."

The rows of food vendors were overwhelming, even though Alissa knew of everyone who was selling food.

"Maybe skipping breakfast was a mistake," Alissa said with a laugh. "I want to eat every single thing all at the same time."

"I don't think that's possible." Dane snorted, coming to a stop next to the first stand, which was serving pizza. "But I understand your desire to try."

Alissa laughed. "Why don't we do a round first before settling on something? Then we can share?"

Dane took her hand, smiling. "I get the feeling that we'd share food regardless of our plans, Miss 'Can I Taste That'?"

She gasped in mock-offense, putting a hand to her chest. "What do you mean? I never, ever eat off of your plate at every single restaurant we go to."

The couple laughed. Alissa was notorious for sneaking bites of Dane's food, even if she claimed that she didn't want any when they ordered. Dane had gotten used to it. It was just a part of their relationship at that point.

They held hands as they made a loop through the food area. All of the mouthwatering scents mingled together, drawing them from booth to booth like magnets. Dane made a note of all the places they wanted to go to on his phone, and when they got back to the beginning of their loop, they divided the list and conquered it. Alissa was tasked with getting Hawaiian pizza from Pauly's Pizzas booth and sliders from The Crab's.

She got the pizza first since she knew she'd linger around The Crab's booth and talk to Hannah if she was free. The line for The Crab was long, as Alissa expected, but they had extra help today.

"Hey, Alissa!" Hannah said. Instead of wearing her usual t-shirt with The Crab's logo on it plus denim shorts, she was in a pretty, long skirt and an off the shoulder top, a flower in her hair. She was off to the side, guiding people through the line.

"Hey! You look amazing," Alissa said. "Not working the booth?"

"Nope. I have the rest of the luau to relax since I did all of the prepping and drove over here." Hannah looked over her shoulder at her dad, who was manning the register. "I'm supposed to be meeting Luke in a bit."

"Oh?" Alissa grinned and Hannah's cheeks colored.

"Yeah. He asked me the other day." Hannah adjusted the flower in her hair. "He's really nice."

"I'm glad you guys hit it off." Alissa stepped forward in line. "What should I get for Dane and me? He's fine with anything but I want to get him the best you have."

"We have a sampler platter—definitely get that. It's all of the sandwiches, burgers, and tacos we have in mini-form. If you cut each one in half, you can taste everything."

"That sounds perfect. Thanks, Hannah!"

"No problem. See you on the dance floor later!" Hannah disappeared into the crowd.

Alissa ordered the sampler platter, which took up a whole tray filled with mini versions of the menu, and made her way to the picnic tables lining the beach. Dane was easy to spot, sitting at the table closest to the water. He was looking out onto the water, where people were surfing, unaware of her. Alissa took a second to study him, her heart fluttering. He really was handsome, especially like this: relaxed and happy, the small lines fanning out from his eyes slightly deeper because he had been smiling all day.

"I have about fifty different things to taste on this tray," Alissa said, sliding the tray from The Crab onto the table, followed by the huge slice of pineapple and ham pizza.

"Wow, that's more than I thought it would be," Dane said. "Here's the poke bowl and kalua pig."

The two didn't waste any time, digging into the food. Alissa started with the kalua pig, which practically melted in her mouth. Then she moved onto the poke bowl, which was all her favorite parts of sushi in an easy-to-eat bowl. The raw tuna tasted incredibly fresh, making the whole dish even better.

Then came the sampler from The Crab, which Dane was already digging into.

"Start with the huli huli chicken sandwich," Dane said, pointing to a sandwich he'd cut in half. "It's amazing."

Alissa picked up the half of the sandwich that he'd left behind and bit into it. An explosion of flavor burst across her tongue—a hint of sweet, a hint of salty, a hit of fruity.

"So good," Alissa said, holding her hand up in front of her mouth while she finished chewing. "Wow. I hope they bring this back onto the menu at some point. I want a full size of this."

"Same here."

They devoured the rest of their food, watching people learn how to surf as they did. Some people wiped out immediately, barely able to get up on their boards, but others managed to get on their feet and ride the waves.

"We still need to have a surfing lesson. Michael's more than ready to teach us," Alissa said with a smile.

Dane's cheeks colored, but he smiled back. "You're not going to laugh at me for barely being able to get up on the board?"

"Of course not, because I'm also going to be

slipping off my board left and right." Alissa laughed. "We'll be total beginners together."

"That sounds like a good plan. I'll give it a shot if we're together."

He reached across the table and squeezed her hand, filling Alissa's chest with warmth. She understood his hesitation, but he was getting past it for both of their sakes. Embracing the things that were outside of his comfort zone. Alissa couldn't have been prouder.

They spent the rest of the afternoon wandering around the party, talking to friends and playing some of the games. Everyone stood on the beach to watch the sunset, the band playing some Hawaiian tunes in the background. Then, the dance floor started to fill up.

"Dance with me?" Dane asked, squeezing Alissa's hand.

"I'd love to."

Dane pulled Alissa onto the dance floor, right as Hannah took to the piano to play a few songs. Alissa rested her head against Dane's shoulder as they swayed to the beat, inhaling the clean scent of his shirt mingling with the cologne he always wore. The luau was everything she wanted it to be and more.

* * *

Luke looked out over the luau, tucking his hands into his pockets. Most people had wandered over to the dance floor now that it was dark, the decorative fairy lights hung up around the open space. People were dancing to the upbeat music, some in pairs and some in groups. To his surprise, he recognized a lot of them, the regulars that he'd come to know over the time he was there. He could see himself missing them when he went home. Missing all of Blueberry Bay, really.

His eyes drifted over to Hannah, who was laughing and talking with a girl he vaguely recognized. They looked his way and smiled, waving. Luke waved back. He wondered if she'd thought about the scholarship or told her dad about getting in. She seemed happy, so if she had, it must have gone well.

He grabbed another mai tai before coming back around to where Hannah was. She always looked pretty, but she was particularly beautiful tonight. Her dark hair was loose in waves around her bare shoulders, the flower in her hair fluttering in the wind. The way her brown eyes lit up when she saw him made his heart flutter uncontrollably in his chest.

"Hey," Hannah said.

"Hey." Luke gave her a brief kiss on the cheek, which made both of them blush. "You sounded great when you were playing earlier."

"Thank you! I was nervous at first but it got a lot easier as I went on." Hannah nodded toward the water. "Want to walk down by the beach?"

"Sure."

Luke tentatively took her hand, then threaded his fingers in hers with more confidence when Hannah grinned up at him. They walked in comfortable silence until they reached the part of the beach where the water lapped up on the shore. Hannah kicked off her sandals and Luke followed suit, dipping their toes into the tide.

"I told my dad about the scholarship," Hannah said.

"You did?" His heart skipped a beat. "How'd he react? What did you decide on?"

"He was so supportive and excited for me." Hannah's smile spread across her face, dimples appearing in her cheeks. "He wants me to go."

"That's amazing, Hannah." He squeezed her hand.

"I couldn't have asked for a better reaction." Hannah bumped him with her hip. "I hope you don't mind me following you."

"I don't mind whatsoever. It's going to be great." The slightly unsettled feeling he'd been carrying thinking about what was going to happen between them at the end of the summer disappeared. "I know you'll love it there. There are so many different kinds of people and amazing things to do. And we'll come back to Blueberry Bay. I love it here too."

Hannah stopped, resting her head on Luke's shoulder. "I'm so excited. I can't wait."

Luke looked out onto the ocean, illuminated by the moon. He couldn't remember a time he'd been so happy and thrilled for the future.

"I can't either," he said, sliding an arm around her waist.

ALSO BY FIONA BAKER

The Marigold Island Series

The Beachside Inn

Beachside Beginnings

Beachside Promises

Beachside Secrets

Beachside Memories

Beachside Weddings

Beachside Holidays

Beachside Treasures

The Sea Breeze Cove Series

The House by the Shore

A Season of Second Chances

A Secret in the Tides

The Promise of Forever

A Haven in the Cove

The Blessing of Tomorrow

A Memory of Moonlight

The Snowy Pine Ridge Series

The Christmas Lodge

Sweet Christmas Wish

Second Chance Christmas

Christmas at the Guest House

A Cozy Christmas Escape

The Christmas Reunion

The Saltwater Sunsets Series

Whale Harbor Dreams

Whale Harbor Sisters

Whale Harbor Reunions

Whale Harbor Horizons

Whale Harbor Vows

Whale Harbor Blooms

Whale Harbor Adventures

Whale Harbor Blessings

The Chasing Tides Series

(set in Blueberry Bay)

A Whisper in the Bay

A Secret in the Bay

A Journey in the Bay

A Promise in the Bay

A Moonbeam in the Bay

A Lullaby in the Bay

A Wedding in the Bay

For a full list of my books and series, visit my website at www.fionabakerauthor.com!

ABOUT THE AUTHOR

Fiona writes sweet, feel-good contemporary women's fiction and family sagas with a bit of romance.

She hopes her characters will start to feel like old friends as you follow them on their journeys of love, family, friendship, and new beginnings. Her heartwarming storylines and charming small-town beach settings are a particular favorite of readers.

When she's not writing, she loves eating good meals with friends, trying out new recipes, and finding the perfect glass of wine to pair them with. She lives on the East Coast with her husband and their two trouble-making dogs.

Follow her on her website, Facebook, or Bookbub.

Sign up to receive her newsletter, where you'll get free books, exclusive bonus content, and info on her new releases and sales!

Made in United States
North Haven, CT
17 July 2024

54886877R00137